Snack

Emme Burton

Snack
Emme Burton
Copyright 2016

Disclaimer: This book is a work of fiction and any resemblance to any person, living or dead, any place, events or occurrences, is purely coincidental. The characters and story lines are created from the author's imagination or are used fictitiously.

The following products/entities along with others mentioned in Snack are trademarked: iPhone, Jamoca Almond Fudge, Star Wars, L'Oreal, Stay-Puft, Legoland, Rainforest Café, and Spaghettios.

Editors: Lauren Schmelz and Janine Weathers, Write Divas Editing
Cover Design: © Sarah Hansen, Okay Creations.
Author Photograph: Dana Colcleasure
Formatting: Polgarus Studio

To my very own Wookiee, Jasper.
Love you so much, boy.

Snack Playlist

"Thinking of You" Katy Perry

"Better Man" Pearl Jam

"Here Comes Your Man" Pixies

"I Just Don't Know What To Do With Myself" The White
Stripes

"Linger" The Cranberries

"Ice Cream" Sarah McLachlan

"The Imperial March" (Darth Vader's Theme) *Star Wars
Soundtrack*/John Williams

"Are You Gonna Be My Girl" Jet

"U.N.I." (*One Take* EP version) Ed Sheeran

"Feel Good Inc." Gorillaz

"Sugar, We're Going Down" Fall Out Boy

"We Belong Together" Mariah Carey

"Thinking Out Loud" Ed Sheeran

"The One That Got Away" The Civil Wars

"Fall for You" Secondhand Serenade

"Not A Bad Thing" Justin Timberlake

"I Won't Tell A Soul" Charlie Puth

"The One That Got Away" Katy Perry

"When I Was Your Man" Bruno Mars

"Love You Madly" Cake

"Rude" MAGIC!

"Chandelier" Sia

"Photograph" Ed Sheeran

"Some Type of Love" Charlie Puth

Prologue

I enjoy the middle part of stories more than the rest. If asked, I would tell anyone my favorite installments of (NERD ALERT!) *Star Wars* are: *Episode V The Empire Strikes Back* and *Episode III Revenge of the Sith*. In fiction and movies, I like the unfolding, the figuring out, the discovery. I tolerate beginnings because, well, every story needs exposition and backstory. I'm less a fan of the end. Because is it really ever the end? I waver between craving the resolution and wanting to know what's next—because even at the end there is always something next.

By contrast, in my everyday life, I yearn for the answer, the resolution. I can't stand things left undone. Oh, I can procrastinate with the best of them but I like my conflicts resolved. Maybe it has something to do with the way I grew up, but I wish for the proverbial happy (or, at least, content) ending.

That being said, I'm also a huge hypocrite. I don't have resolution. I have the illusion of resolution. I'm learning to live in the *middle* of life, appreciating the beginning and not knowing the end. Endings seem painful, even when happy. I tend to ruminate about endings—obsess, if you will. I wonder about how it could've been better. I think about how it could've been worse. I think about what would've happened if Anakin had shared some of his darkest demons with someone other than Emperor Palpatine. I ponder if any of my beloved antiheroes and tragic romantic characters (think Eponine from *Les Misérables*) could've had a happy ending. They certainly are the most interesting characters in books, movies, and plays. Full of repressed emotion and angst. So dramatic. If they are my example, then interesting life or love equals uncertain, sad, and tragic.

In real life: I hate these people. I'm not interested in the drama queens with their broken engagements and tales of unrequited love and bitterness. It seems unearned and fake.

When it happened to me, I discovered it was not a very attractive real-life option.

Chapter 1
2014 – Mountain Climbing

If I didn't already think I was a fucking weirdo, this confirms it. Who the hell else fantasizes about Darth Vader to get off during sex?

It's really effective ninety percent of the time. If I think about Darth Vader (or sometimes, to change it up, Severus Snape) I can climb Orgasm Mountain like a Sherpa. Not this morning. Right now, Henry is between my legs working me over, and I can't get out of base camp. I know what I have to do. I don't want to have to do it, but Henry could get a tongue sprain if I don't soon. I let the picture of *him* enter my mind.

Marcus Snackenberg.

Snack.

The crack of a starter pistol fires in my mind, and I sprint to the summit of Mount O.

Ooooooooh, my God! Yes! A delicious swirling clenching overtakes me as I imagine Snack, not Henry, making me feel this

3

way. I may need a hit of oxygen after I reach the summit. Fastest ascent ever. My body is warm and tingly and well pleased.

Henry looks up from downtown. He looks pleased with himself. Almost smug.

Me? I feel a little guilty. Like a traitor to myself. And Henry. Really, he made a spectacular effort to get me off and the whole time I was thinking about another guy.

Dammit! Snack is my past.

I really don't know if Henry is my future.

Reflexively, I smile down at him. Henry pushes himself up a bit, rests his head on my stomach, and sighs. I run my fingers through his perfectly-coiffed-even-though-it's-morning product-laden dark brown hair.

Physically, sex with Henry isn't bad. It isn't earth shattering either, and lately we've just been getting each other off without actually fucking. Just lots of blowies and tongue-lashings of the little man in the canoe.

"Minnie?"

"Yeah, Henry?"

"How was that? I'm gonna guess it was pretty spectacular because it sounded like you really enjoyed it."

God, he's arrogant sometimes.

"It was awesome, Henry." I'm not lying. It was awesome. His tongue did a great job. Unfortunately, it ultimately wasn't what pushed me over the edge.

Henry, my roommate/activity buddy/sex partner, falls asleep immediately, snoring through his stupid fucking hipster mustache. I mean, it feels pretty damn good when he's giving me a *cat bath*, but in everyday life the 'stache is

4

just so cliché. Guess what, guys? Not everyone looks good with facial hair. Some of you just look like homeless lumberjacks.

From my description of our relationship, it should be pretty obvious Henry and I haven't DTRed: Defined The Relationship, yet. We met eight months ago and started hanging out. The sex was easy and uncomplicated and somehow he wound up moving in. Like, his shit kept accumulating here and then he said, "It doesn't make sense to pay rent on two apartments."

And I said, "Well, you might as well move in." It was more like a business deal, but it's better than being alone, I suppose.

We don't even come close to talking about our relationship—ever. I think we're both keeping it loose for reasons from our past. I know I am. Let's just say, I don't have too many positive experiences with love or trust.

I love four people in this world, but I only really trust about 2.75 of them. The 0.75 is my older brother. It's really a stretch to trust him at times. Snack is in there in the love part. Henry doesn't even figure into the equation. I keep trying to make him fit and push Snack out. I never was any fucking good at algebra.

My phone rings, essentially saving me from thinking about my strange ritual for achieving orgasm and distracting me from my guilt. I mean, it's not overwhelming guilt, but sometimes I feel like maybe I'm not putting in enough effort. Henry's nice enough, gainfully employed, good-looking. So maybe he's a bit commitment averse, but he's fine with pleasuring me for as long as it takes. Even if I am thinking about someone else. That's OK, I'm positive I'll revisit it later. The guilt. Maybe the odd orgasm thingy, too.

My phone rings again. I can tell by the "Luke, I am your Father" ringtone that it's my dad.

After pushing my comatose roomie from between my legs and onto his side of the bed, I grab my iPhone from my nightstand and swipe the screen.

"Hi," I say breathlessly.

"Minnie Mouse, it's Dad." He says this *every* time he calls me, even though I know it's him and he knows I know it's him.

"I know—"

"You sound like you've been running. You OK?"

I could honestly say, *Actually, mountain climbing,* but I don't. Instead I reassure him. "I'm fine."

"Minnie, you need to come home." Dad's tone is low and commanding, which is unusual for him. Generally our conversations are light. He's never really been effective at demanding anything from my siblings or me.

My brothers' well-being immediately springs to mind. "Why? Is everything OK? Are the boys OK?" As the only girl in the family, I've always felt maternal toward my brothers, even though I'd never admit it.

Dad sighs heavily. "It's Snack."

When Dad called I knew what I had to do—Wookiee and I caught a train from the city right after work. I went back to the apartment and threw a few things in an overnight bag, stuffed Wook into my purse, and hauled ass to Union

Station to make the 5:04 train to Downers Grove. I waited until I was aboard to call Henry.

"Hey, just wanted to let you know I'm going home to visit my dad and a family friend who's having a crisis."

"You don't want me to *go* with you, do you?"

I shake my head. What? What kind of half-assed offer of support is that? He's never met my dad or my brothers or even shown any interest. I don't think this trip is the time.

"No, I don't think so," I reply flatly.

"OK." Henry's voice over the phone becomes distant and starts breaking up, "So, I'll see ya." The call drops when we go through a tunnel.

That's it? Not even, "I'll see ya *soon*." What's worse, it doesn't even piss me off. Henry may not know it yet but I think our relationship has just been defined. I hate to admit it , but I'm pretty sure we're just fuck buddies. Fuck buddies that share an address.

***

This is pretty much my favorite place in the world.

The entire world.

The northeast corner of Main and Burlington in Downers Grove, Illinois in the courtyard of the train station.

Why?

One word. You've probably already guessed it.

Snack.

Childhood best friend, love of my life, loss of my life, biggest regret, one that got away. Snack.

I've been in love with Marcus Snackenberg since before

I knew what love was.

I look in my large purse, lock eyes with Wookiee, my Yorkie, and tell him, "We're here, Wook. This is it. Time to make the jump to hyperspace." There is no other way of describing being back home. Wookiee, appropriate to his name, gives me a throaty growl. Yes, his name is Wookiee. What else would a *Star Wars* obsessed nerd girl like me name a miniature, seven-pound version of Chewbacca?

We moved to Downers Grove when I was six. It wasn't exactly a happy or well-planned move. My father was thankfully and magically, I believe, good friends with the Snackenberg family. And I, by lucky default, got a friend.

Marcus Snackenberg.

No one ever calls him Marcus. Not even his parents. He truly is a snack. A visual cupcake of a child that grew into a decedent layer cake of a man. And nobody, not one person in our town could resist gobbling him up when he was around. Not when he was a kid, and from the last few Christmas card pictures I've seen, probably not now, either. As a kid, grownups would pinch his cheeks and stroke his hair and, like unknowing prophets, tell him what a lady-killer he was going to grow up to be. As we got older, girls, hell, even soccer moms, practically stood on their fucking heads and did the splits to get just a tiny bit of notice from him.

So, here I am, standing at my favorite place in the world. Glued to the spot after getting off the train and staring at the familiar café cattycorner from my position. I'm having difficulty getting myself to move.

Paralyzed and gawking at the sign above the door that reads *SNACKS*, I hope against hope to catch a glimpse of the man that has always shared that name. And has always owned my heart.

For the past fourteen years, every time I've come home on the train from downtown. I do it. Winter. Spring. Summer. Fall. I just stand here for a few moments across from the shop. Imagine him there. Dream for a few seconds about sitting inside with him like we used to. Sometimes a tear will sneak out of one of my eyes. God, that pisses me off more than anything!

Fucking crying?

Over what?

A wish that will never come true. More like a dream that started, and then I finally woke the fuck up.

Each and every time I scold myself. "Fucking crybaby. Snap out of it! Stuff that feeling away. He was never really yours." I know with a high degree of certainty that today, I will see him.

I want to.

I don't want to.

I'm a fucking mess, if you want to know the truth. And I'm freezing. It's cold as hell in January in Chicagoland. I can feel Wookiee shivering inside my purse. I sense he's going to start barking loudly to go in where it's warm, soon.

All I can think is *Snack is back*!

What will it be like? I haven't seen him in years. I've, at times grudgingly, held on to so many feelings about him. My heart harboring too many unrealistic hopes that I keep

EMME BURTON

tamped down. A friend. Remember, Minnie, he just needs a friend.

Standing here, with snowflakes swirling around me while the street lamps flickering in the twilight seriously consider turning on, I'm transported back to the first time I ever stood in this spot.

Chapter 2

1988 – Welcome to Downers Grove

The summer before pre-kindergarten, my dad lost his job. And my mom. Not in that order. We lost my mother first. Oh, we didn't *lose her* lose her. We knew where she was. We just weren't sure if she was ever coming back to us.

A year later, very suddenly, we moved from just outside of Boston to my dad's hometown, Downers Grove, Illinois. We traded one bedroom community for another. Like upgrading when your older sibling goes to college. I don't know if moving was an upgrade, so much as a necessity. It seemed to be an upgrade for my brothers. To this day, I'm still not sure about my dad and me.

I don't know why we're standing here. We got off the train and now Daddy has us just standing outside the train station. All of us, my older brother, my baby half brother, Sid and me, not moving and looking at some restaurant across the street. I can see my breath.

"Clippy, what's going on?" I ask my big brother.

My dad interrupts. "Baby, his name isn't Clippy or Clip, it's Clif or Clifton." I don't know what Dad's problem is. I've always called my brother Clip.

"I like to call him Clip, Daddy," I say and press my lips together.

"It's no big deal, Dad. I like it, too," Clip interjects.

"Yeah, I do, too," Daddy says and smiles big down at me. "It was your mom that always insisted we call him by his correct name. I guess we can call him Clip as much as we want, now." He reaches down with his big hand and rubs my hair through the stocking cap on my head.

Baby Sid starts crying. His cheeks are red and he has shiny snot running out of his equally red nose. He must be cold, too.

"Come on, kids," Daddy says and we follow him across the street to the restaurant.

My father, Gil, is… *was* an engineer for a large company in Massachusetts. One day he came home from work and never went back. The day before that, my mother went out for groceries and never came back. As much as we asked, Dad never told us *exactly* where our mom went. He'd tell us something vague, like she's on a trip or visiting her parents. Dad was never much for lengthy or heavy discussions. If we pushed or cried, he left and went to his room. Maybe he was trying his best to hold it together in front of us. I'd creep up and listen at the door. All I could make out was a strange sound like a ghost being strangled. I was too chicken to go into his room and find out what the noise really was, but I'm pretty sure he was crying. Before we moved to Illinois, I would sometimes hear him on the phone talking to someone—begging them to come home. No one else was missing from our house, so I can only guess it was my mother on the other end of the line.

In Massachusetts we lived in a big old house that smelled like a cozy fire even in the summer. It had two stories with windows that rattled when the wind blew and floors that creaked with every footstep. I loved it. I loved every noise the house made. Daddy used to tell me during storms that *there's nothing to be scared of.* I would always reply with an *I know.* The noises actually comforted me. I was sad to leave my one-hundred-fifty-year-old house and all the noises and smells I loved. For a long time it was just Daddy, my older brother, and me in that house.

Then one day like a bolt from the blue, my mother showed up at the door, handed a baby to my father, and left. All she said was "His name is Sid. He's not yours." Then poof! Gone. I remembered it all clearly, because I stood at Daddy's side, holding the leg of his jeans. She never looked down at me. Not once. She never asked to see Clip or me. She delivered her package and left. That's how I got my half brother. Dad accepted him without argument, gave him our last name, and legally adopted him. As a kid you never realize what an amazing thing that is to love a child that isn't your own.

It was only years later I found out that my mother was very ill. Mentally ill. After leaving Sid with us, she was arrested a few months later for vagrancy and public intoxication. She didn't have to go to jail. The judge ruled she was too sick and sent her to an institution. Of course, it's not *called* an institution; it's called a hospital. It's been years. I don't think she'll ever leave.

The visit from my mother and the arrival of Sid set everything in motion. With no job, a big house, and three kids, my dad decided to move us back to his hometown, Downers Grove. Clippy told me we'd been to Downers Grove before, but I honestly didn't remember. All I knew was we were packing all our things, moving far away, and going to live with my Mimi in her basement, and I wasn't allowed to bring my pet hamster, Eggroll, with me because we were going on a plane. It was pretty much the embodiment of a nightmare for a six-year-old.

"Where are we going, Daddy?"

"Inside. To that café over there. It's called SNACKS and my friends own it. We can get something to drink and warm up," Dad tells me as he opens the door.

The welcoming smell of cinnamon and coffee and warmth immediately surround me in a cocoon of sensation I'm sure I will never forget.

"Gil! Gil Cooper! What are you doing?" A pretty lady with her long blonde hair pulled back in a red bandana rounds the counter. "You were supposed to call when you got to O'Hare. I was going to send Robert to get all of you."

When she gets to us, she hugs Daddy really hard and then kisses him on the cheek. The lady smiles, but her eyebrows pinch together and her eyes are wet. To me, her face looks happy and sad at the same time, so I can't tell what she's thinking. Then she laughs a little. Grown-ups are so weird.

I've never seen anyone but my mom hug my dad. And I can't

even remember that very well. Why is this lady hugging and kissing my daddy?

I think my dad is almost crying because I hear him sniffle and then his shoulders drop. His voice sounds funny when he says, "Colette. It's so good to see you. You have no idea how good it is to see you. I didn't want to trouble Bob or you with coming out to get us. The train was fine. The kids like the train."

The train was really cool, but I was so tired I fell asleep and missed seeing anything out the windows.

"Oh, Gil, look at these adorable boys," the pretty lady chirps excitedly after touching Sid's cheek and then squatting slightly to look at Clip and me. I'm about to correct her and tell her I'm a girl when she calls over her shoulder. "Snack! Come meet the Coopers!"

A yellow-haired streak comes out from behind the counter, nearly knocking the Colette lady over. "I'm right here, Momma. You don't have to yell." *It's a boy. It must be Colette's boy. He looks like he's Clippy's age. He has hair the color of his mom's and big blue eyes that look like—fun. Like he has all kinds of ideas for fun… and maybe a little trouble! I like him already.*

"Come meet Mr. Cooper and his boys. Gil, this is my son, Marcus or Snack. Everyone just calls him Snack."

Why does she think I'm a boy?

My dad says, "Uh, Colette—" But he doesn't get to finish because the boy cuts him off and comes to stand right in front of me.

Looking me straight in the eyes he says, "Momma, this isn't no boy… This is a girl."

"What?" The pretty lady's eyebrows jump up.

"Yes," my dad says. "I have two boys and one girl, Colette. These are my boys, Clifton and Sid. My daughter's name is Minnie. I guess I could see how you'd make that mistake. They are all sort of dressed alike." I look at Clip and Sid and realize we all have on similar clothes. Thinking about it, we probably looked like three little convicts. Denim overalls. Chucks. Winter coats. Mittens and stocking caps. All of us in blue. I don't like pink, so I guess Daddy just put me in the same things as the boys. I never really thought about it before. I didn't care. Until just now.

The yellow-haired boy hasn't stopped looking at me. Even though it makes me feel a little uncomfortable, I don't want him to stop. He hasn't paid any attention to Sid or Clip.

"See, Momma, I told you she was a girl. She's too pretty to be a boy." Nobody had ever called me pretty. Not anyone in my whole six years of life. Not that I can remember. Boys don't talk about pretty things and I was always only around boys. Suddenly, the boy pulls off my mittens and shakes my hand. "Hi, Minnie! My name is Snack."

My name is Wilhelmina Jane. Who does that to a kid? Wilhelmina Jane. There are so many horrible combinations of names you can make from that. Shall I elaborate? Willie J. Minnie Jane. It only got worse after the media started with the *JLo*/Hip Hop nickname thing. The list goes on. Then add my last name—Cooper. Yup, you got it. Minnie Cooper. For real. This was never a thing when I was a kid— only in the 2000s when Mini Cooper automobiles were introduced and that damn *The Italian Job* movie came out. Now, my name is a big joke.

Snack helps me with my coat and hat, throwing them on a nearby chair and then, without warning, hugs me! This family sure likes to hug. "I'm glad you're FINALLY here, Minnie," Snack tells me throwing his arms up in the air dramatically. "Let's go play!"

I look up at my dad. He nods that it's OK to go with Snack. I hear Snack's mom say, "Oh, I'm so sorry, Gil. She just... Why are you dressing that sweet little thing like a boy? Overalls? A pixie haircut? Really, Gil?"

Daddy sighs and I hear him tell her, "I know, I know. It's just I don't know much about girls. And she doesn't like pink or Barbie dolls."

Dad was right. I didn't and still don't care for the color pink. Living in a family of boys didn't set me up for much exposure to girl stuff. I preferred to play with Hot Wheels and Legos and my Star Wars action figures. The other little girls at my day care in Boston thought I was strange. I wound up hanging out with the boys—just like at home.

Snack and I go over to an area on the other side of the café, away from the windows that face the train station. There's a fireplace and it's much warmer. My new friend has a huge toy box with all of my favorite toys and then some. Not only does he have Legos and Hot Wheels, he has electronic football and Micro Machines, too. Clip been begging for some of those. He gives me a tour of all his stuff and when he finally stops talking, he says, "What do you want to play?"

I know I should say something. I haven't said a word; he's done all the talking for us both. This yellow-haired boy is so loud and busy and interested in me. That's new for me. Nobody ever asks me what I want to do. Daddy's always so busy with Sid because he's a baby. The last time I saw my mommy I must have been invisible because she acted like she didn't see me. This boy doesn't think I'm invisible. He's so... pretty and nice. I don't know why I can't talk to him. I talk to my brothers with no problem.

I'm about to open my mouth to tell him I don't know when Snack points at my chest and says, "What's that?"

I look down at the pocket of my overalls. A small, furry, golden head with beady eyes looks up at me. Busted! I look over my shoulder to see if my dad is watching. "That's Eggroll, my hamsta," I whisper.

"Your hamsta? Oooooh, your hamst-ER. I like the way you say that."

I had no idea at the time my Boston accent was funny or different. As a matter of fact, I thought Snack sounded pretty funny, too. He never teased me about it. He'd just laugh and try to say things the same way. Twenty-six years after our first meeting my accent is a distant memory, only appearing when I'm very tired or drunk or both.

Snack laughs a little too loudly. "Eggroll? That's a funny name." I turn my head again to see if Daddy's looking. I could get in trouble for hiding Eggroll in my pocket and bringing him on the plane. Dad and I agreed I would give him away. I packed him up in his cage and took him to school, but then I just couldn't do it, so lied and told Dad I gave him to my kindergarten teacher. I didn't. I threw out his cage and kept Eggroll hidden in a box in my room until it was time to leave. Then I snuck out with him in the bib of my overalls.

I take Eggroll out and hold him for Snack to pet, making sure to shield the meeting from my dad's view.

He smiles at Eggroll and then me. "Why do you call him Eggroll?"

"Because he's the size and col-ah of an eggroll and he smells yummy. At least, I think he smells yummy."

Daddy must have sneaked up behind me because I jump when he says, "Wilhelmina Jane Cooper! Is that what I think it is?"

Snack instantly comes to my defense, saying something like, "Don't be mad," "She just didn't want to be alone, and I'll help her take care of Eggroll." Just like that, Magic Snack, my hero in blue jeans and Keds saves the day for the first, but not the last time, in my life.

"Please, Mr. Cooper." Snack has his hands folded together like he's praying. His eyes are big like a puppy's. My dad seems to be powerless against Snack, too, because he caves and agrees that I can keep Eggroll since he must be a super hamster to survive a cross-country trip on a jet.

"Minnie, we'll get a new cage for Eggroll tomorrow," Daddy tells me with a half smile. "I swear you kids run right over me." I let out a sigh of relief. Thanks to Snack that went much better than I thought it would. Daddy hardly ever gets mad at me, and I hate to disappoint him, but giving up Eggroll was too hard.

My brothers are half-asleep at a table in the café. Sid is propped up at an angle in a high chair; his head bobbing up and down. Clip's hot cocoa is barely touched. He has his hand around the mug, but he's staring into space. The chime on the door rings and I see my Mimi has arrived, and Daddy abandons the Eggroll discussion. He hugs Mimi and talks to her, occasionally pointing back at the boys and me. I don't know Mimi very well. She sends us nice Christmas presents, but I've never spent more than a day or two with my grandma. We never see my mommy's parents at all.

"I didn't know Miss Janice was your grandma," Snack says.

"Yep, that's my Mimi." I didn't really know her as anything other than Mimi. Janice? Who's Janice?

Snack asks a natural question next. "Where's your momma?"

"She doesn't live with us anymo-ah. She's in a hospital. She's sick," I reply matter-of-factly.

My six-year-old reasoning was unconsciously protective. Just the facts. No judgment. It is what it is. It would only be later that the feelings of loss and betrayal about my mother would surface.

Snack accepts my explanation with a shrug and an upbeat "Oh," and we decide to make a Lego pen for Eggroll on the floor of the café. He probably needs the exercise since he's sort of fat. Eggroll is used to hanging out in my overall pocket, since I trained him over time, but not as long as he's been in there today. We nearly have it finished when Daddy interrupts our play and tells me to gather up my stuff and wake the boys up because it's time to go.

Snack runs to his mom and asks loudly, "Momma, can my girl spend the night at my house?"

"My girl? Who's his girl?" Mimi looks at my dad with her face all scrunched up.

Standing right next to Snack, I turn quickly to look at him and scratch my head.

Colette Snackenberg puts her hands on Snack's shoulder and beams. Her smile is huge—I like it. "Your girl?" She looks over at me and then strokes my chin. Her hands are so soft. "Do you mean Minnie? Is she your girl?

"Yeah," Snack says and puts his arm around me, pulling me closer to his side. I like his arm around me. Everything in me tells me I should always be this close to him. He's fun.

Colette glances over at Daddy and Mimi and then laughs. They join in. I don't know what they're laughing about. There's nothing funny about what he said. I want to stay with Snack.

If I'm honest, from that moment on… I never wanted to be away from him.

"He's never acted like this before," Colette says to the other grownups and then bends down to address Snack. "It's a school night."

Snack isn't backing down. "Friday, then?"

"Sure," Colette answers. She shakes her head a little and sort of smiles and frowns at the same time. "What's gotten into you, Snack?"

Snack was very bossy with me and about me from the start. I never let anyone boss me around, but for Snack, I rolled over like a beagle begging to have her tummy scratched.

I've come to suspect that Snack claimed me from that moment on. Claimed me, owned me. Ruined me for anyone else. At six years old.

Chapter 3
2014 – I'm Going Home

Dad's call? The one after Henry gave me my toe-curling, Dark Lord, tongue bath? Went something like this: "Snack's wife is dead."

A rush of air left my lungs after unconsciously holding my breath, and with relief I blurt out, "Oh, thank God!"

"What?" my father replied, aghast.

"No, Dad, I mean... Oh my God, that's horrible, but I thought you were about to tell me *Snack* was dead."

Dad sighs. "He might as well be. The poor guy is really torn up. It was sudden. He's been back home for a while. I can't believe this is happening to him again." Dad briefly relays the story of Megan Snackenburg's brave struggle against breast cancer after having her last child, remission, then the unexpected recurrence, and death from complications of chemo.

I'm stunned and think *holy shit, not again* but only hear my breath hitch, in a failed attempt to stifle a sob. The odds of lighting striking a person twice in one lifetime are one in nine million. The odds of tragically losing the person you love twice are much lower, but it doesn't make it less horrible. Snack's odds suck.

It's like Dad knows what I'm thinking in that sob when he says in a thick voice, "Yeah, the guy can't catch a break."

This makes me laugh inappropriately inside for half a second before I reprimand myself. In many ways throughout his life because of his looks and charm, Snack did nothing *but* catch breaks. But in his current situation, just like fourteen years ago—not so much.

Since I remain quiet my dad continues, "There wasn't a visitation or funeral. Megan, just wanted a memorial and they did it back in her hometown about a month ago. It was small and private. Snack's mom didn't even know about it. Colette's pretty torn up about that, but she'd never say so. Snack's moved back to Downers Grove. You know he's got those little kids and needs to be closer to his mom."

It strikes me that Snack's move back to DG is not unlike the one my father made years ago.

"So, Min, can you come? The guy's a fucking mess. Some days he doesn't get out of bed all day. The days he does he wanders around like a zombie. I think Snack would really like to see you."

I swallow a few times and reply, "Yeah, I'll be there. I'll come right after work."

***

SNACKS has been through several iterations since its establishment. It had been a soda fountain and a wine bar in the past, but I've always known it to be a coffee shop. I should really just walk across the street and into the place. I'm being such a freaked out girl-pussy right now. I check on Wookiee in my bag. Even in his little red plaid snow jacket, he's trembling. He looks up at me and chuffs a breathy bark requesting to "Please, let's get warm."

I lean down close to his cold nose, and after kissing him say, "Don't worry, you'll be warm in a minute." Then I look up again.

There's a man wearing a black beanie, sporting a full blond beard, and talking to two little kids inside the café. He looks familiar, but larger, more filled out than I remember. From the way he moves, I don't think it can be anyone else but him.

The man glances up and just stares out the window at me. From across the street, through the large pane glass window with the fat snowflakes floating around me, our eyes lock. Nobody else in my whole world looks at me that way. The visual connection is confirmation that it's him.

Snack.

I suck in a breath of cold, bitter air. It stings my lungs, triggering a coughing fit. I hold my hand to my chest as I cough and try to clear my throat. As I regain my composure, I wipe my watery eyes. *That was graceful.* Snack cocks his head and a gigantic grin breaks across his face. He holds up one finger, indicating for me to hold on, says something to the little kids, and rushes to the front door of the café.

If something could happen in slow motion and super speed at once, it is Snack making his way out to me. The way his body moves, his muscles straining his sweater as he walks, and the stride of his step paralyze my senses. But before I know it, he's standing right in front of me. I haven't seen him for eight years. I've kept up through my dad, Colette and, I'll admit, a little social media stalking a few years ago, but for eight years he's just been a 2-D image on a Christmas card photo.

"Minnie? Is it you?" His voice breaks with emotion. "Is it really… my girl?"

He hasn't called me "his girl" for fourteen years. Since the night I told him to quit calling me that. I've missed it. Being called somebody's. I love the richness of his voice. The way its warmth wraps around every word like he's chosen it just for me. My heart instantly recognizes it and slams itself against my ribcage over and over, trying to get to him. "Minnie?" He steps closer when I don't move.

I realize I haven't responded. I probably haven't blinked. He sounds like Snack, but this man looks a bit different—not as "light" as the Snack I last saw in person—exhausted, beat down. I finally, after what must have been a lifetime, nod my head and ineloquently puff out, "Uh-huh."

"You've got to be freezing, Min." His frosty breath drifts in the air as he speaks. "I know I am." He crosses his large arms across his wide chest to stay warm, and I pull my eyes away from the face I've missed so much without allowing myself. Even through his gunmetal gray cable knit sweater, I can tell how much buffer he is than be used to be. Snack steps a bit closer, unfolds his arms, reaches out, and places this hands on my upper arms, rubbing up and down.

Freezing? Is he kidding? Warmth I thought I'd forgotten fills my chest. I exhale three times quickly. What's happening? Why am I hyperventilating?

I finally let out a deep laugh. "Yeah, freezing." It's just a small lie, but I'd say anything to keep him touching me.

When I look up and into Snack's face, his eyes stop me. His eye color always seemed to be dependent on the amount of cloud cover on any given day. If the day was overcast or about to rain: navy. If there was not a puff of white in the sky and blue skies for miles: ice blue ringed with black. "Like a Siberian Husky," I used to tell him. Tonight, they looked swollen with fatigue and stormy gray, even though he's smiling.

"Liar!" he whispers loud enough for me to hear. Liar? That I'm just the opposite—getting warmer every moment I'm near him? As if reading my mind he says, "Just seeing you again has warmed my cold, sad heart." I immediately recall how Snack could always say things to make me love him without even trying.

"How are you?" I ask because, a) I can't say what I'm really thinking, which is "Oh my God, you are still fucking gorgeous and perfect," and b) it's the socially acceptable thing to say to someone that's experienced a loss.

Snack presses his lips together and then smirks, "Better, now that I've seen you."

Swoon.

Colette Snackenberg taps on the window from inside the café. She mimes shivering by rubbing her hands on her arms and motions us with a wave to come in. Snack takes my gloved hand in his bare one. I glance at our entwined hands and then look up at his profile as we make our way across the street. When's the last time I held his hand? It feels the same even through my gloves. Electricity or something shoots up my arm and that familiar warmth engulfs me, starting around my heart and filling my entire chest. I hadn't realized a void had developed there until just this moment when I suddenly feel wholeness I haven't in years.

Stepping into SNACKS, I stomp the snow from my boots on the welcome mat. I take a second to appreciate the smell. The same cinnamony smell welcomes me, just as it did when I first stepped in the store when I was six. No other place on earth smells like SNACKS. After the train station courtyard, I'm pretty sure this is my second favorite place. Snack begins brushing snow from my shoulders. He surveys me from head to toe. I've said approximately five words since I saw him, but we don't appear to need them to communicate. After he pulls off my gloves and stuffs them in my coat pockets, much like the first time we met, I reach up and whisk some snow from his beard. Snack grabs my hand and leans his face into it. I cup my palm around his jaw and glide my thumb across his silky whiskers to really feel them and him.

"You look like nobody owned you, as my Mimi used to say." I bite my lip and half smile.

Snack's eyes well with tears. Then he closes them, presses his lips together, and swallows a couple of times. I don't know if he's smiling or suppressing a sob. "Nobody does... anymore."

Dammit! I've said the wrong thing. I've never been good at emotional talk. Perhaps the result of living in a house full of boys.

I fumble an apology. "Sn-Snack, that was insensitive."

"No, it's OK. It's true, and I *could* always count on you to bottom line it."

"I'm so sorry about Megan. She was always really nice to me. Dad told me what happened."

Snack's eyebrows rise. "Really, because we haven't talked in a long time."

"I know. I just… I couldn't. But I'm here now. I'm sorry I couldn't come to the memorial."

"Yeah, Megan specifically didn't want a funeral. She didn't want anything really, but we compromised on a memorial, only if it was very small. Her parents swooped in after she died and set it all up. Honestly, I was a mess. I had all I could do keeping the kids going. They're amazingly resilient, but you never know with them. Sometimes they're just fine, playing videogames or coloring and the next they're crying and falling apart. I'd like to say I handled it better than they did, but I didn't. Grief is like that. It's messy and nonlinear."

"I really am sorry." There's no truer sentiment to be expressed.

Snack turns into my hand and softly kisses my palm. A sensation I'd forgotten, but only felt in my dreams, returns with so much magnitude my first reaction was to let go of him. As much as I like it, it also feels *too* good and uncomfortable being so intimate in public with a man who just lost his wife. I try to pull away, but the sweet, sad sparkle in Snack's eyes and the warmth of his skin won't let me. That and the fact that Snack reaches up and holds my hand closer to his face.

Still stroking his beard, I giggle awkwardly to lighten the mood. "Seriously, what's with all the fucking facial hair?" And just like that, any insecurity I harbored about seeing Snack again after so long and under terrible circumstances, are gone. We are Snack and Minnie again.

"Watch your mouth, Cooper." Snack smirks and nods toward where the little kids are sitting close by. "Some things never change."

I've always had a mouth like a sailor. Snack was more of a *clean* dirty talker, dropping panty-scorching verbalizations without swearing at all.

I chuckle and pick up on his not-in-front-of-the-kids nod. Bugging my eyes out at him, I say, "I mean… *jeepers creepers*, Snack. What's with all the facial hair?"

Snack shakes his head and rolls his eyes. "Wow, Min, even when you say jeepers creepers it *still* sounds like your cussing." Snack removes both our hands from his face, but continues to hold my hand. Still skin-to-skin, our connection is becoming almost overwhelming.

"R-r-r-r-r-r, r-ooof!"

"Minnie, your purse is barking." Snack chuckles.

"Oh my God, Wookiee!" Wookiee responds with a pitiful whine. I was so overwhelmed by Snack I forgot about Wook hanging out in my purse. I shake myself out of my Snack-induced coma and open my purse to a wide-eyed, shuddering puppy. "Oh, baby boy, you must be a little frozen chicken nugget by now." I place my purse on the closest table and pull off my coat. Snack takes it from me and throws it over a chair. I leave my beanie on, unsure how my hair looks underneath.

Wookiee reprimands me with a few more hoarse half-barks as I lift him out, nuzzle, and kiss him. A Yorkie in a lumberjack outfit must ring some sort of universal cuteness alarm because I'm surrounded before I know it. Colette grabs Wook and me and hugs us tight in her arms. Snack follows suit and engulfs us in his massive hold, all six foot three of him. The Snackenbergs are a family full of huggers—you know, nose to toes, every bit of your body smashed against the other person. No modesty gap or, as my ever-so-classy brothers would call it, *boner gap*. A Snackenberg hug was the best kind of hug and I was the lucky recipient to have… *four* of them? Two pairs of small arms belonging to an unmistakable golden-haired girl and boy squeeze my legs. I smiled down at the two of them. Snack's children. I've only ever seen their pictures on Christmas cards. Every year I knew to expect a cute card with their happy faces smiling wide for the camera. Just not this last Christmas.

"Can we play with your puppy?" the boy asks.

Snack reaches down and gives the little boy's hair a ruffle, "Hey, buddy, give Minnie a second." The little boy's face falls. Wookiee wriggles, trying to free himself to get to the boy.

"Sure, you can," I reply. I'm instantly met with a smile

that rockets me back to this same place in 1988 when I was smuggling a different animal in my clothes. And this little boy? He's a carbon copy of his dad. Great! Another tiny lady-killer stalking the streets of Downers Grove. I'm about to put Wookiee on the floor but think better of it. We *are* in a restaurant, after all. "Colette, is it OK? For Wookiee to be in here?"

Colette surveys the place. Apart from us, there are a couple of college kids in the corner probably home on winter break, and a guy by the window with a guitar, writing things in a notebook.

"It's fine, honey. I don't think there are any health inspectors out on a snowy Friday night. Usually as long as dogs are held they can be in here, so go ahead. Let the kids play with him. They could use some fun!"

Snack is shaking his head, "Do you always show up here hiding pets in your clothes?"

"Evidently, yes."

I plop Wookiee on the floor and he breaks into a chase after the kids back to the play area by the fireplace. He's as happy as they are for the novelty of a new playmate.

Once the kids and Wook are occupied, I become aware that Snack hasn't backed away from our hug and is resting his hand on my lower back, his inner forearm grazing my side. His touch unnerves me. He leans down and whispers in my ear, "I wanted to introduce you to my kids—"

"Aiden and Sofia, right?" I turn my head an inch to purposefully feel more of his breath on my face. I close my eyes briefly and absorb the tingling it causes before adding,

"But you call Sophia Fifi."

Snack stays close, but seems surprised I know the kids' names and Fifi's nickname. "How did you?"

I don't understand why it should surprise him. Doesn't he know?

Then his face breaks into a large toothy smile as he realizes, and we say in unison, "Christmas Cards."

SNACKS is only open for another hour, and my dad should be here soon to get me. As a matter of fact, I wonder why he didn't come get me at the train station like he said he would? I hope he's OK. I shift my gaze out the front windows, craning my neck in search of him. I should probably check my phone, but for some reason I ask Colette.

"Colette, you talk to my dad, right?" Colette blushes a little then and Snack snorts. Weird. "He said he'd meet me at the station, but he's not here yet."

"Oh, Minnie, honey, I forgot with all the excitement of you arriving. Gil called. He's on his way. The snow drifted against his tires and he had to dig out. I told him I'd be on the lookout for you."

Snack raises his eyebrow at his mom. "Wait. You knew she was coming?"

Colette grins at me and then at Snack. "Yeah, sweetheart. Gil and I thought you needed a happy surprise." She pats Snack on the shoulder and ushers us to a table away from any of the remaining customers. "What can I bring you both?"

I start to protest that Colette doesn't need to wait on me, but she insists sweetly that it's no problem. At first, I order a grande latte but change my mind after Snack orders a hot chocolate. I'll have to persecute him for ordering the drink of a tween girl, but it sounded good the minute the order left his naturally pouty and now pink-from-warming-up-after-being-outside lips.

"OK, I'll be right back with those," Colette chirps. She turns to leave but spins back around and tilts her head. "It's so good to see you two together again."

Colette and Snack share an unspoken moment before he says, "Thanks, Mom." His voice cracks and he clears the thickness out of his throat. He smiles. "Are you sure, Mom? You weren't always so happy to see us together."

Colette turns and walks away, waving away Snack's comment with a flick of her hand above her head. "Yes, I'm sure. Even if I know you two together usually meant trouble."

Chapter 4
1994 – Jamoca Almond Fudge

Colette is completely, unequivocally right. The combination of Snack and me equals, or should I say, equaled, trouble. Not like bad criminal trouble. More like mischief. It's what turned us into best friends.

Soon after Snack and I first met when we were kids, we kidnapped Snack's neighbor's cat. Our reasoning for doing so was sound in the minds of a couple of six-year-olds. The kitty was always crying at the neighbor's door and it was getting cold outside. We figured the neighbor didn't love it, so we took it in. It lived secretly in my bedroom for a week. Snack and I saved food from our dinners to feed it. It wasn't until my dad smelled the stifling stench of cat urine coming from my room and discovered my body riddled with a bazillion fleabites. We had to evacuate our house and have it fumigated. That was when we realized *why* the neighbor's cat lived outside.

Another time we gathered up all the kids on Snack's cul-de-sac and the big chocolate lab Rollo that lived near us and took off for the park without telling a grown-up. At the park we found a big beehive hanging from a branch. In the *Winnie the Pooh* books, Pooh is always eating honey and says it tastes so good, so we convinced Pierson, the booger-eater that lived on the corner, to knock the hive down so we could eat the honey. We didn't figure on the bees. They swarmed around all the other kids who didn't run off when the hive hit the ground. They were stung so badly an ambulance had to be called. It was lucky for us that when our parents found Snack and I hiding out with Rollo in Snack's bedroom closet. They were more relieved than angry that we had the sense to bolt after dropping the hive and not get attacked by killer bees.

When we were thirteen we set Mr. Gary's, Snack's neighbor, lawn on fire on the Fourth of July. There was a really bad dry spell that summer and no one was allowed to water their lawns or flowerbeds. All the yards were crispy and crunched under our feet when we walked over them. It wasn't our fault that his grass caught fire. It was the Fourth. How could you not wave around a sparkler or two or twenty?

The fire wasn't *that* bad. It only took the *small* fire truck to put it out.

In every case, we got punished. Worse than being spanked, our parents grounded us from seeing each other. They couldn't have picked a more punitive sentence. Many mornings, Snack would be at my house when I woke up. I spent every afternoon and evening before the streetlights came on with him. There was rarely a day we didn't hang out. It killed us to be apart from each other. As far as I was concerned, Snack was my best friend and the best thing to happen to me.

The one that sticks out the most was, as it is known in our families, the *Lake Geneva Incident*. It wasn't about being naughty. None of our hijinks really were. No, the Lake Geneva Incident was about Snack not wanting to leave me and me not wanting him to go. It was 1994. Kids didn't have cell phones. There was e-mail, but Snack's parents didn't have a computer at the cabin. Long distance was expensive and not the same as being in the same room. How were we supposed to talk to each other when we were going to be separated for eight weeks?

There are suitcases in various stages of being packed all over the place in Snack's living room, boxes full of non-perishable foods and swim bags with suits and flippers sticking out of them. Snack and I are playing Sonic the Hedgehog 3 and narrating the game to avoid talking about the fact that we're not going to see each other for a long time. At least that's what I'm doing. He might be doing it to distract me because I'm totally kicking his ass.

"Snack, we're leaving for Lake Geneva in forty-five minutes. Don't wander too far away!" Colette yells down the staircase.

"Mooooom!" Snack drags out her name in a moan and then sarcastically adds, "I'm twelve years old, woman. I don't 'wander' anywhere anymore. I know where I'm going. I have direction!"

I giggle. I don't know anyone else who can get away with

saying the things Snack does to his mom.

"All right, Mr. Focused." Colette always knew how to respond to Snack's snark.

Snack cocks his head, makes a goofy face, and jerks his head toward the door. He suddenly shuts down our game, which I object to by opening my mouth in shock.

I recover in a heartbeat. "What? I was winning,"

Snack grabs my hand, pulls me off the floor, and out of his house.

Once outside he drags me over to our bikes that are laying in the front yard as usual.

"Let's go get ice cream." Snack hops on his bike. When I don't move fast enough, he eyes my bike and then me.

We only have a short amount of time to get to our favorite ice cream parlor The Frosty Station, down by SNACKS.

Concerned, I bite my lip. "Are you sure?"

Snack nods. A clever gleam in his eye sparkles when he says, "Yep."

We head down the street toward the ice cream place, but when we get to the end of the block, Snack starts pedaling really fast—like lightning fast. Like someone-is-chasing-him fast. And then, he turns in the exact opposite direction of The Frosty Station. Evidently, we aren't going there at all. I pedal my BMX bike as fast as I can, but I'm shorter and smaller than Snack, and I have to work harder to stay with him.

When I finally catch up, I yell, "Snack, what the hell *are you doing? We're going the wrong way! And my legs are aching." I rub my calf."You made me pedal so fast."*

Snack just shrugs. "I decided I wanted to go somewhere

different. I'm tired of The Frosty Station. I wanted Jamoca Almond Fudge. Only one place to get that—"

"Baskin-Robbins," I finish his sentence. "But that's pretty far away. On the other side of the highway."

Snack only nods and starts pedaling faster again.

"Hey, Snack. Um, can you slow down a little," I gasp. "You act like you're being chased. What are you running from?"

I'm not really thrilled about biking on these bigger roads with more cars. We've never biked this far from home before and the vehicles are too close. Whenever a truck goes by I'm afraid I'll lose my balance, fall off, and get crushed. Snack slows enough so I can move along next to him and we bike a little longer silently. He doesn't look at me either. Finally he answers my question.

"I'm running away from vacation."

"What do you mean? 'I'm running from vacation.'"

Snack doesn't clarify and I'm starting to get annoyed. He's acting weird. Maybe this isn't just about going on vacation. Snack points out that we have arrived at our destination. We lean our bikes against the mailbox out front and go into Baskin-Robbins. Snack gets his Jamoca Almond Fudge cone and I order Daiquiri Ice in a cup. When I dig into the pocket of my jean shorts for change, Snack grabs my wrist.

"I got it."

Again, weird. He's never paid for anything for me before.

I tilt my head and say, "OK." and take a bite of my Daiquiri Ice. It's sweet and sour at the same time, refreshing after our long, hot ride. Snack and I sit on the curb next to the mailbox and quietly enjoy our treats. Snack is acting so strange and I'm *pretty sure he, no—we, actually, are going to get in big trouble for biking so far from home. I don't even know how long we've been gone. When I finish my last bite, Snack takes my dish and spoon out of my hand and places them on the curb next to him.*

"I'm running away from vacation for as long as I can because I'm not excited to go to Wisconsin. I'm not excited about leaving Downers Grove for the summer. I'm… I don't want to leave… you. My girl." Snack stumbles over the last few words, and I almost can't believe what he's saying. But I feel the same way.

I gulp and then cover my awkward excited embarrassment with a laugh, mostly because Snack's words feel different. Serious. He's never talked to me like that before except when he first called me his girl when we were little. That was ages ago. Through my giggling I tell him, "You're gonna be in big trouble. Correction: We're gonna be in trouble!"

Snack laughs nervously, too. "I know." He gets serious again and brings his face really close to mine. I can smell the Jamoca on his breath. "And I don't care if I get in trouble." And with that, Snack kisses me. His lips press firmly against mine. They are cold from the ice cream and warm underneath. And sweet. So sweet.

I close my eyes. This might be the best feeling in the world. Better than ice cream or when Darth Vader admits he's Luke's father or… I don't know. I lose the ability to retain rational thought, I think. The kiss is not a peck like my baby brother gives me on the cheek. It's not a gross openmouthed kiss like in the movies, all slobbery and spitty. It's just right.

As I pull away drunk from the kiss and slowly open my eyes,

I see before me flashing red and blue lights. No, not fireworks, although that's what I thought for a second with the feel of his lips still heavy on mine. No, my first kiss was just witnessed by Downers Groves' finest. A DGPD patrol car with its cherries blazing pulls next to us, and a police officer steps out and comes toward us.

"Marcus Snackenberg? Minnie Cooper?" His expression is stern and flat.

"Yes," we answer simultaneously.

The police officer shakes his head and chuckles, which is a relief. Perhaps we're not going to get too much grief. "You two have your folks worried sick. Come on, get your bikes and throw them in the back."

Snack whispers to me, "You're dad is going to be so mad! He'll be like Obi-Wan Kenobi!"

"Snack, Obi-Wan is one of the good guys. You call yourself a boy? You know nothing about Star Wars! Besides, if anyone has a scary father it's you. Your dad is Boba Fett."

"What do you mean?"

"I mean he's cold, steely, and barely talks."

Snack shrugs. "True."

Snack and I return to his house in the aforementioned police cruiser. His parents and my dad are waiting in the driveway. We're greeted with hugs, tears, repeated scolding, and warnings that if Snack wasn't already going away we would've been grounded from seeing each other for a long time.

Snack whispers, "That's why I ran. This vacation is like a giant grounding. Trapped in a moldy old cabin with giant mosquitos, no Nintendo, no computer, and no Minnie." I hear him and so does his mom, earning him a swat on the rear.

The Snackenberg's car is packed and ready to go, with the exception of Snack's stuff. Colette stands at the open door of the car, tapping her foot. "Snack, go in and get your bag so we can leave.

Mr. Snackenberg has already started the ignition. His irritation at the delay appears to outweigh any relief he had at finding us when he bellows out the window, "And HURRY UP!"

My dad looks down at me and shakes his head. When the police officer unloads our bikes, Dad rolls Snack's into the garage.

I stand frozen, replaying the entire afternoon in my head, especially the kissing part. I rub my lips with my fingers.

When Dad comes back he cocks his head and squints at me. "You OK, Min?" I nod and Dad drops it. He walks over to Colette shaking his head and holds his hands up by his ears palms up.

Snack runs out of the house with a bulging backpack over his shoulder. He stops for a moment in front of me, looking me dead in the eyes.

My heart is beating so fast, and I can't stop thinking about the way his lips felt on mine. I know he's thinking about our kiss, too. I wish I could kiss him again right here, right now.

Snack reaches down and loops his pinky around one of mine and says softly, "My girl."

I hope nobody else heard. I hope his words are only for me.

The moment is interrupted when Colette yells from the car,

"Snack, come on! I want to get to the lake before dark."

"Coming!" Snack turns away and moves to the car.

Colette isn't finished. "Did you go potty already?" she asks him loudly.

"Yes." Snack responds without embarrassment.

"Really? You weren't in there very long."

In true Snack style, he gets the last word. "Yes, Mom, I can pee fast. It's the wonders of having a penis!"

Before getting in the car, Snack turns and winks. "It's true. It's amazing to have a dick!" Thank God his parents are already in the car.

Laughing, I roll my eyes in an exaggerated way. "You are a dick!"

Snack lets out a huge snort and says, "Yeah, but you love me anyway." Then he puckers his lips, blows a kiss at me, and disappears into the car.

He has no idea how correct he is.

Chapter 5
2014 – Snow

Snack reaches across the table and grabs my hand, weaving his fingers in mine. It's a familiar move. It's the way Snack used to hold my hand—with our fingers all tangled up together.

"God, the Lake Geneva Incident…" He shakes his head like he can't believe the crap we used to pull. "Some first date, huh?"

I gape in disbelief. "That was a date?"

"Hey, I paid for the ice cream." Snack chuckles. His laugh is good to hear and infectious.

I giggle along with him. "And practically got me arrested."

Snack's laughter dies and he takes my other hand. He gives me a tight squeeze and lowers his voice. "After a *very* memorable first kiss."

I feel a jolt of excitement rush up my chest and plummet down to my belly, making me squirm in my seat. I look down at our tangled hands and a vision of our bodies doing the same flashes in my mind. I feel a naughty grin creeping onto my face.

What am I doing? This man just lost his wife. He can't be flirting with me? I shouldn't be thinking what I'm thinking. And what about Henry? Whatever he is… Boyfriend? Roommate? I felt lousy just visualizing Snack while I was with him this morning. Now I am canoodling. Snack just needs a friend. Settle yourself, Minnie. I quickly wipe what I can only guess is an inappropriate expression from my face.

"Yes!" I can barely get out the word as I look up from the table and into his heavily lidded, navy blue eyes. Navy blue eyes that look a little wet. Snack gulps a couple of times. "Min… My girl… I've miss—"The front door of the café flies open and a large gust of cold air invades the warmth of the place. Snack looks up and I twist in my seat to see what's happening.

My father, wearing a significant dusting of snow, comes through the door and stomps clumps of the wet, fluffy stuff off his boots. I guess it started getting bad out there. I was so wrapped up in Snack, I hadn't noticed.

Colette runs from behind the counter to greet my dad. "Gil, you're covered! What in the world is going on out there?"

"The snow is getting worse. I think we're in for a blizzard. I parked the El Camino down the street and walked a block. Look at me!" He holds his snowy arms out to the side. "I'm a snowman."

The two of them laugh together. It's so great my dad has such a good friend here in town. Colette brushes the snow off my father with a dishtowel from her back pocket. She and my dad let out a whoop as snow flies all over the entryway and begins melting and dripping down Dad's face. Colette, almost reverently, wipes the melted snow away from his cheeks with the towel. He smiles at her as she does, and I feel like I'm intruding on a private moment. Dad eventually looks up from Colette's face and meets my gaze. He blinks way whatever fog Colette consumed him with. Maybe I did catch him in something. He leans down and says something to Colette quickly.

Looking back at me, he yells, "Mouse!" Mouse is Dad's shortened version of his nickname for me, Minnie Mouse.

"I don't know why he calls you that. You're nothing like a mouse," Snack states. I tilt my head and press my lips together. Mouse just goes with Minnie, but there's no need to explain.

I remove my hands from Snack's and get up to go see my father. By the time I get to him, Colette has helped him remove his coat and hat so I can hug him without getting drenched.

"Welcome to Chiberia! Well, technically, I guess Downers Grove is Outer Chiberia." Dad wraps me in his big arms and squeezes me tight. He must be hanging around with Colette more than I thought, because this is a Snackenberg hug, not a Cooper hug. He kisses me on the forehead and says, "Looks like you and Snack are catching up."

"Yeah, a little," I reply.

"Can't wait to do more," Snack says from behind me, causing me to jump a bit in Dad's arms. "Hey, Gil!" Snack sticks out his hand for my father and shakes his hand while holding onto Dad's elbow in an affectionate manner. All the patrons that were in SNACKS when I arrived have left. I didn't even notice anyone exit; I was so caught up in reminiscing with my old friend. Colette has flipped the open sign to closed and turned off most of the lights now except for the ones behind the counter and in back where the kids are playing.

"Snack." Colette places one hand on Snack's shoulder and one on my dad's. "It's getting late, maybe we should get the kids home to bed?" Snack and my dad say, "Yes, good idea," at exactly the same time. Bizarre. Why would Dad answer that question?

"I just need to close up," Colette says, "and then we can take off."

"You know what, Mom? Why don't you let Min and me clean up and shut down?"

"Really?"

"Sure, you and Gil can take the kids in the mom-mobile."

"The 'mom-mobile?'" I try hard to squelch a cackle.

"Yes, I drive a minivan," Snack says. "Don't start with me, Cooper. I have kids."

My cackle turns into a full-blown giggle fit when I wave my hand and say, "I'm not saying anything." Snack directs his attention back to his mom and my dad. "Like I was saying"—Snack shoots me the stink eye—"Mom, you can take the van. Minnie and I will come home later in the El Camino. If that's OK with you, Gil."

"Then I can pick you up and we'll go home, OK, Dad?" I add.

Dad nods at Snack. "Sure, that sounds fine. But"—He chews on his words—"Umm, Minnie Mouse, I'm sort of… *staying*… at Colette's." Dad blushes with this confession.

I look to each person in the room for some sort of explanation.

Colette pipes up, "Gil has been helping out taking care of the kids along with Snack and me so I can work at the café and Snack can start looking for a new job. It's just been easier for Gil to stay at the house."

I think it's odd that Dad didn't mention this vital information on the phone. Exactly how long has Snack been home in Downers Grove? And how long has Dad been *staying* with Colette? Something's up. I can't put my finger on it, but I don't think I'm getting the whole story.

Dad stutters, "Yeah, um… I'm helping and you know our house is big… And Sid hardly ever comes home since he moved out and… Uh…"

"So, where am I staying?"

Dad replies, "We'll figure it out once you guys get to Colette's. Depending on the storm. Maybe we'll all just stay there tonight and figure it out in the morning."

"Fifi! Aiden! Get the toys picked up and come on. It's almost time to go," Colette calls to the kids in the back of the café. Wookiee tails them, barking and jumping with joy at his new playmates. He stops right at Snack's feet, sits, and looks up at him. Snack reaches down and picks him up. Wook let Snack hold him without growling or whining. He *never* lets Henry hold him. He barely allows Henry to pet him. Evidently, Snack can also charm beasts as well as women. "Wow, since when did you become The Yorkie Whisperer?"

"Minnie, did you forget how crazy awesome I am with animals. Remember how much Eggroll loved me? Huh?"

He's killing me. Great with kids *and* animals. I could have sworn I didn't have a biological clock, but I do because he just wound it up.

Snack holds Wookiee like a small furry football as he tells his kids to get their coats and hats. The kids go and get their jackets from the table where they were sitting and put them on independently using the "preschool flip" method. Running back toward us, Aiden pleads. "Puh-lease, can Wookiee go home with us?" Fifi bounces up and down with her hands together, chanting, "Please, please, please, please."

I'm saved from being the bad guy when Snack tells them, "Wookiee needs to stay with his mom but you'll see him soon.

"Tomorrow." I promise them. "You can have breakfast with him." Aiden jumps up and down at the news. I can still detect a bit of a pout on Fifi's face.

My dad assists Colette with her coat and the two of them hustle the kids out the door, but only after Aiden and Fifi both give Snack and Wookiee kisses. Just before they are about to exit, Aiden runs back and hugs me around the legs.

No words. Just a leg hug and a big mini-Snacklike smirk. His sleepy, beautiful blue eyes shine up at me.

"Wow, when did *you* become The Kid Whisperer?" Snack asks.

"Did you forget how crazy awesome I am with… No, I got nothing. The only kid who ever liked me was Sid and he sort of had to, brother and everything, you know."

"Not the only kid, Minnie." Snack points his thumb at Aiden walking out the door. "You made him very happy. Well, you and Wookiee here."

Wookiee barks his agreement.

Snack gives Wookiee a rub behind the ears and places him on the floor, and then he turns away and goes behind the counter. I watch Snack's gaze drop to the floor as he pinches the bridge of his nose between his thumb and forefinger.

When our parents and the kids are gone, I start picking up dishes that are left around the café and bring them back to the sink behind the counter. Snack puts away cups and plates from a tray. "What else can I do to help?" He hands me a cloth. "Wipe down the tables?"

Snack is being so quiet. Too quiet. I break the silence awkwardly. "You've got gorgeous kids. Aiden looks a lot like you, but Fifi…"

Snack sighs and rubs both hands over his face, wiping away a little moisture from his eyes with the last swipe. "Looks like Megan?"

I nod. Oh my God, he's talking about Megan. His dead wife, Megan. "I know. It's hard sometimes. Seeing Megan in her little face. I love it. I hate it. Sometimes it makes me ache and other times it's a precious reminder. The truth is, Minnie… I'm a wreck. A walking freaking disaster. I left my job and moved us back to Downers Grove thinking they could have more stability. I didn't really think it through. I just couldn't be in that house anymore. And work. I didn't want to see everyone's pitying faces at work. Now, here I am, living at my mom's house and looking for a new job. I mean, we're fine financially, we'll be OK, but… what am I doing? How am I going to raise these two kids on my own?"

He tries to hold back the sadness lumped in his throat. But I hear it in the tremble of his voice. He swallows back some tears and turns away, wiping down the espresso machine. His shoulders move up and down, followed by an exhausted sigh. I go to him and from behind him, take the rag from his hand. I place it on the counter next to us, and turn him around to give him my best impression of a Snackenberg hug. I press the side of my face to his chest and hear his steady heartbeat while I hold him in my arms. It should feel wrong to be this close to him—this intimate— but it doesn't. It feels… right.

I sense the tension leave his body after a few deep exhalations. I relax, too. Removing my cheek from his chest, I tilt my face up, resting my chin on his substantial pecs. Snack drops his head and holds my gaze. His eyes are wet, but he blinks more tears away. He searches my eyes and then his eyes drop to my lips. I'd love to kiss his full lips and take away some of his pain, but it would it be inappropriate. Snack leans down a bit more and I push up onto the balls of my feet. If he kissed me now there's no way I would or could stop him. My heart is totally overruling my brain. We're a breath apart, the kiss inevitable when…

Snack's cell phone rings and vibrates in his pants pocket. I can feel it only too well! Instead of kissing me, Snack laughs, shakes his head and says, "Perfect!"

Only making enough room between us to reach into his pocket to get his phone. He looks at the name on it and then swipes across the screen to answer the call.

"You've got Snack. Talk to me." Snack winks at me when he answers with his patented phone salutation. I haven't heard it in so long, but it still makes me smile. I'm still reeling a bit from the "almost kiss." I think I can make out my dad's voice on the other end. "Really? That bad, huh? You got there OK? OK. No, I think you're right. Hang on."

Snack puts his hand over the speaker of the phone and says, "It's your dad. He says the storm's getting really bad out there. He doesn't think we should go anywhere. It was a nerve-racking ride to my mom's house and it's only a few miles. The El Camino has rear wheel drive. It's not great in the snow. Are you OK with staying here? With me? Overnight?"

Am I OK with spending the night with Snack? Alone? My heart says, "Hell, yes!" I just wish my logical conscious would shut up.

"Stay?… Here?" I squeak. How are we going to sleep in the café? "Where are—"

"Don't worry," Snack interrupts. "I've got the perfect place." He returns his attention to the call while rubbing his hand up and down my back. I'm more tired than I thought and his touch is so soothing, I could purr. "Gil, you still there? We'll stay put. Tell Mom to call me in the morning."

As Snack says good-bye, I put my head back on his chest and reach up to grab and twirl a piece of my hair that is poking out of my beanie. I start twirling it fast. As a matter of fact, I have my "full twirl" on. It's the thing I do when I'm getting tired—I twirl my hair.

Snacks hand comes to mine and stops my twirling. "You're tired."

"How do you know?"

"You're twirling your hair. You only twirl when you're sleepy."

"You remembered." I smile into his chest.

Snack laughs—it's a deep, sexy rumble I feel through his chest. "Of course, I remember. It's a weird thing."

Once again, I look up at him. Snack's no longer laughing. He's quiet, intense. He runs his hand across the top of my gray angora beanie and removes it. A look of surprise crosses his face, his eyes pinching together. "When did you become a suicide blonde?"

I open my mouth to protest and say, "What?" Then I recall I am a blonde now. Suicide blonde is an expression I once used to describe Snack's old girlfriends. He slides a piece of my hair between his thumb and forefinger and rubs it. He whispers, "The softest thing… my suicide blonde."

Chapter 6
1999 – Suicide Blondes

You'd think after Snack kissed me that summer when we were twelve that would have been it. Childhood sweethearts finally admitted their love for each other and voila! Happily ever after. If only. No, as Shakespeare said, "The course of true love never did run smooth." But at twelve, who really knows how to tell if what they're feeling is love and what "running smooth" looks like in their life? I finally convinced myself Snack forgot about kissing me, and I certainly wasn't going to bring it up and make things awkward.

Through junior high, Snack and I walked or biked to school together. We hung out after school, playing video games or making mix CDs. I went to school events and dances in a group that included Snack and Clip and whatever guys they were currently running with. Oh, and let's not forget the girls that were fascinated by them. Every time I turned around another girl was throwing herself at Snack. Even though he kissed me that one time, it seemed that I was just another one of the guys. I was confused. Why would he kiss me and call me his girl and then just go back to being friends?

By the time we were freshman in high school, the kiss was a faded memory. For him, at least. Snack dated other girls. Every single one of them a blonde. And tall. And stacked. I was none of those things.

I'm five foot four. I have blue-green eyes and my original hair color is medium ash brown. I know this because I've had a plethora of hair colors since college and my roots came in a lot darker than they did when I was a kid. Out of curiosity a couple of months ago, I took my picture from high school to the supermarket to figure out my real color. It matched L'Oréal 5A Medium Ash Brown. Not that I want to go back to it. I like my current blond color. It's definitely *not* average.

The point is, the weird thing about Snack and his blondes was, after his *dates*, he'd come to my house and hang out with *me*.

I didn't think too much of it at the time.

"Minnie, Snack is here!" my dad yells up the stairs from the front door.

"Send him up to my room," I yell back.

I hear Dad's footsteps and a second pair coming closer. "Your room!" he bellows.

I yell in my dad's face just has he comes through my door. "Jesus, Dad, it's only Snack!"

My dad whispers, "Oh, right." Like Snack and I have never hung out before. Like this is a new thing. Snack turns his body sideways and slips past my dad to go sit on my bed.

My dad frowns and adds quietly but firmly, "Door open."

I shake my head and grin. Then when he doesn't budge, I nod to get him to go. He backs out of my room and leaves my door cracked. Snack is just my friend. We hang out all the time and nothing happens. Not that I'd mind if something did. But it never does. Never will.

Then one night when Snack happens to have arrived at my house before I get back from a late night of working on the school paper, I overhear a conversation between Snack and Clip and it gets me wondering.

I don't mean to eavesdrop but then I hear Clip say, "What about Jacksy?" The distinctive clicking of game controllers in use echoes through the room. When I look around the corner, they're facing away from me, sitting on the sectional, and playing Mario Party.

Snack moans and says, "Jennifer Jacksy? No, no way. She's chased me so hard ever since freshman year. And she's a bookmark."

"A bookmark?"

"Yeah, a girl that guys use to mark the place that they left off when they break up with their girlfriend. That's Jacksy. It's terrible, but in Jacksy's case, true."

Clip replies with a "Ha!" and then says, "So, give it to her, man. She'll love it. She always does."

I know for a fact that Clip has banged Jennifer Jacksy. I know because I heard them. Clip had a party one weekend my dad had an overnight business trip. My God, it was horrible listening to them on the other side of the wall.

"Penny Jenny? Really, Clip?" Snack groans.

"Sure. Have some fun. Harmless fun. It will only cost you a penny."

I decide right then and there my brother is sort of an asshole.

I'm about to march in and tell them both they are complete assholes and that's no way to talk about a girl when Snack changes the subject.

"Beside, Clip, that's not who I want. You know who I want to be with." Snack tilts his head and nods back toward the hall where I am. I take a few steps back and hide behind the corner in case he turns around. Who is he talking about?

"That will never happen. Not unless you are going to stop fucking around with your blondes and get serious... And you're too fucking young to get serious."

"Yeah," Snack mumbles in a low and resigned voice I can barely make out.

As I venture forward again, Clip claps Snack on the back. "Dude, what about Charlotte? You know, Charlotte Carpenter, the new girl. That attribute alone makes her a million times more interesting than chicks from around here."

Wow! Clippy used the word "attribute" in a sentence. And correctly, too. Maybe he will go to college someday.

"I don't know." Snack starts and then his tone changes. "Hmm, Charlotte Carpenter."

"Oh, yeah. Charlotte. I can see she's pinging your radar just by the way you say her name." Jesus, Clip can be a slimeball. My brother, the pimp.

I can't stand it anymore. I hate spying on Snack like this. He's supposed to be my best friend, right? I can talk to him about girls, right?

Entering the room breezily, I say, "Did someone mention Charlotte?"

Clip and Snack turn to look at me. Clip immediately returns to the game and says, "Yeah." Snack looks away, guilty.

"Thinking of dating another suicide blonde, Snack?" I snark. I can't help it. It just comes out snotty.

"Suicide blonde?"

"Yeah, you know, those fucking blondes you like to date. The ones that are so gorgeous they make regular girls want to kill themselves."

Snack's eyebrows squish together. "That's sort of harsh, Minnie."

I don't like feeling this way. Snack's mine. But, not really. I can't take it. I gotta get out of here. "Yeah, well—" I bolt out of the room as fast as I can but trying to act nonchalant.

Charlotte Carpenter. She's only been at Downers Grove North High School for three months and already is a coveted cheerleader and member of the student council. She has straight As (OK, in that we're even), blonde, built, and confident. Wears her makeup like fucking war paint and dresses like off the runway. Perfect. Everyday. You'd think the hallways at school had red carpets the way she walked them. And by all appearances she was actually nice, too. Bitch! She made it impossible to hate her.

She was everything I wasn't. Superior. With the exception of good grades and the ability to write, I've always been blissfully average. Right down to my brown, not caramel, not chestnut, hair. Average.

Snack started dating Charlotte, the suicide blonde, the next day.

Chapter 7
1999 – Fall

Snack is with Charlotte. Has been for ten months.

We don't talk to each other at school anymore. Ever. The one time I asked him why, he snapped at me in a terse whisper, "I'm not sharing you. Not subjecting you to those idiots." I didn't know how to respond. Part of me liked it because if he didn't want to share me, it meant part of him still cares for me. Granted he was hanging out with the super popular jock crowd ever since he started dating the fucking perfect cheerleader Charlotte. The popular crowd is a bunch of idiots, anyway. Clip had been part of that crowd, but he was off at college. Snack used to make fun of them with me. Now, he was one of them. I didn't understand why I had to be invisible to Snack at school. Or maybe I wasn't, really. A few times in the fall of our senior year when he thought I didn't see him, I caught Snack staring at me in the hallway. He'd have a look on his face I couldn't decipher. Blank? Angry? Confused? Of course, I couldn't ask him. The unwritten rule was: no talking to each other at school.

I thought maybe he didn't talk to me because it would make her mad. The truth of it was I didn't exist to Charlotte. Oh, she was never mean to me. Then again, she was never nice to me, either. She never displayed any feeling about me. Probably, because she didn't have any. And that's how you know you mean nothing or, more aptly put, are worth nothing to a person. When you don't even register in their life—not for one millisecond. You never pass through their consciousness. Sure, she knew my name. I was Minnie. Clip's little sister, if anything, but she wasn't aware of the history Snack and I had. I guess he never told her that I was his girl first. That he used to practically live in my bedroom every night of the week.

Hell, Snack taught me how to get off on my own. Bet Charlotte would be pissed if she knew that story.

I can never use the bathroom at my house when I want to. Why? Because my little brother is constantly in there, taking a bath and whacking off.

I bang loudly on the door. "Hey, Dr. Spankenstein. What are you doing in there? Trying to reanimate the creature?"

"Just a sec," Sid moans through the door.

Ugh! I hate to picture what he's doing in there.

Watching me in the hallway, Snack leans on the doorjamb to my room. "Oh, give him some slack. Everyone needs some "self amusement" now and then."

I throw my hands up in the air, spin away from the bathroom door, and stomp back to my room and Snack.

"Not me," I declare proudly, shooting him a squint-eyed glare.

"What? You never get yourself off?" Snacks eyes practically pop out of his head and his hands fly to his hair.

"No." My cheeks flame with heat and I know I'm turning bright red. I plop down on the edge of the bed and try to act cool, but inside I'm burning up. This conversation just tipped into the uncomfortable zone. The uncomfortable-because-we're-talking-about-sex zone.

"Like never?" He looks at his feet and shakes his head. I think I detect a crooked smirk on his lips. He leaves suddenly and the next thing I know he's banging on the door to the bathroom. "Hey, Sid! Tug Monkey! I need to piss. Open."

From my perch on the edge of the bed with my thighs pressed tightly together because this whole thing is sort of working me up, I hear the bathroom door open and a whispered conversation between Sid and Snack. Then the door closes.

Snack returns. He stands in the doorway with my electric toothbrush, which he wiggles while holding between his thumb and forefinger.

"Do I have bad breath?" I quickly cup my hand up to cover my nose and mouth and breathe into it. No, breath is OK. Seriously, why is he bringing me my toothbrush?

"Noooooo." Snack shakes his head slowly and smirks. "You are definitely not going to brush your teeth with it." I don't say a word. I'm shocked and intrigued and what I can only think is… horny.

"Here." Snack hands me my brush. His voice gets low. "When I leave, lay back on your bed. Imagine your favorite celebrity or boy band member." I shoot him the stink eye, 'cause I'm not the boy band type. "Then close your eyes, turn that on, *and stick it down your panties."*

I'm pretty sure I gasp, which makes him smile.

"Give me a call later. I want to know what you think. I personally think it's the best way to spend"—he uses air quotes—"'alone time.' You know if you can't have the real thing."

No. I wouldn't know.

Snack knows that and he's rubbing it in. Ha! Rubbing it in. I can't escape the innuendo.

Before he leaves my room, Snack kneels at my feet, runs his thumbnail up the arch, and squeezes my naked big toe. Fucking hard.

I shiver and moan. "Uuuuuuh!"

Snack looks up from his kneeling position, winks, and whispers, "And when you make that sound later today. Remember I'm the one that told you how to get there."

After Snack leaves I stare at the toothbrush in my hand. Stick it down my pants? I couldn't do that? Could I? I guess I'm going to have to use my allowance to get another toothbrush for my teeth.

I get up and lock my bedroom door. With my luck, Sid would march right in without knocking while I was trying this out.

I walk back and sit down on the edge of my bed. Curious, I switch on the toothbrush. The vibration in my hand is enjoyable. Funny, how I never appreciated the sensation before. I run the back of the head of the brush over my arm and the hairs on it stand up immediately. The low-pitched buzz reverberates off the walls of my small bedroom. Surely someone would notice if they walked by. I flip it off quickly. I need a way to mask the sound. *Nobody would believe I was actually brushing my teeth in my bedroom for longer than five minutes. I spy my stereo. Music! Music will drown out the sound. I pop off the edge of the bed and walk over to my CD player. Nobody in the house would suspect anything if I play music I always had blasting from my room. I gently drop the Star Wars Soundtrack onto its perch and snap the lid closed.*

Snack's instructions played in my head over the strains of John William's composition. "Lay down and think about your favorite celebrity…"

I turn all the lights off and fumble my way back to my bed. After stepping out of my sweatpants and wrestling my bra off while keeping my tank top in place, I finally slip in between the cool sheets of my bed with my toothbrush in hand.

I switch the brush back on and move it down my stomach. I slip it under my white cotton panties. At first it just tickles, but when I move it just a fraction of a centimeter down and slightly back, a jolt shoots straight to my core. My legs twitch and relax as sensation after sensation rockets through me. This feels even better than on my arm!

The toothbrush lands on a particularly sensitive spot.

I rock into it. With the "The Imperial March" playing, a vision of Darth Vader standing over me pushes my pleasure higher. Suddenly, the picture of Darth morphs into Snack. My legs tremble and my stomach contracts. Squeezing my eyes tighter, Snack's face is surrounded by a million brilliant colors and shooting laser-like lights. I shudder and exhale a long, loud moaning scream of pleasure. The same sound I made when Snack stroked my arch with his thumbnail and squeezed my toe.

After that, I was addicted. I never again harassed Sid for his "alone time." I also wore the battery out of that toothbrush. Thank you, Snack.

That's how Snack and Lord Vader gave me my first orgasm. Technically, my vibrating wonder brush did, but I didn't get there thinking about Justin Timberlake and his ramen noodle hair. No, the first time I came I was thinking of Snack's face.

***

Like I've said, I always like the middle part of stories better. Any stories: adventure stories, horror stories, romance. I really liked the middle part of my story with Snack in 1999, but I'd have preferred our love story back then didn't start the way it did.

I was used to going to school dances in a group. Usually it was with Clip and Snack and whatever girls they were hanging around with at the time. One of their friends would generally step up and be my official "date" for the evening. They were cordial enough to buy me a corsage, if that counted for anything. I have pictures from every school dance with a different guy. A different guy that never touched me—except to slow dance—never kissed me, never called me, and now that I think about it, never even made eye contact after the dance. Even if I thought they liked me and we seemed to get along during the dance, afterward—nothing.

Fall Homecoming 1999. I didn't have a date the day before the dance, so I figured I wasn't going. The whole

Clip/Snack/Minnie group dance thing was no more since Clip went away to school. I had pretty much given up any chance of going, when Adam Peterson, the photographer from the school newspaper, asked me. We'd always gotten along great, working to meet deadlines. I never even thought about him as a possible date, but he was smart and I could talk to him, so when he asked me I accepted. After all, it would've been the height of patheticness if I didn't go to homecoming my senior year.

***

From the doorway I hear his voice. "It's OK, Adam. I'll take it from here."

Snack is in here. In the darkened journalism room.

I'm sitting on one of the lighted mock-up desks, my homecoming dress hiked up to my knees. The lighting is sort of, well, romantic. Adam is standing between my open legs. He's leaning in for a kiss when Snack interrupts. I freeze.

Adam stills but then quickly looks over his shoulder and says dismissively, "I'm all right, Snack. We're all right, right, Minnie?"

Snack stalks toward us. I can see him as I peek over Adam's shoulder. Suddenly, Snack slaps his hands down on Adam's shoulder and tightens his grip. Adam winces. Snack must not know his own strength.

He clears his throat. "I guess I didn't make this clear. When I said 'I'll. Take. It. From. Here.' I wasn't asking, A-dam." Snack pulls on Adam's shoulder and spins him around so he's facing him now, not me. "Get lost!"

"Snack! Why the fuck are you being so rude to my date?"

Snack snorts and shoves Adam toward the door of the classroom. "Adam understands. Don't you, A?"

Adam turns back to me and shrugs. Just before he exits, he turns around and says, "Snackenberg, you're a psycho. Stop playing with her already. Jeez!" Adam pushes the classroom door open with a loud smack of his palm.

I'm pissed but I'm also so worked up. Snack has always been possessive of me like I'm his toy or a pet, but this feels very, very different.

"What is your fucking problem?" I'm about to push myself off the desk, but Snack rushes me, taking the place Adam had just occupied between my legs. A wave of warmth settles my anger but leaves me confused. And growing warmer by the second. And I don't think it's because I'm sitting on a light box. I think it's because Snack has never broken this kind of boundary with me.

Snack takes my face in his hands and looks me in the eyes for the longest minute in history. I search his eyes for understanding. And just as I realize, Snack's mouth is on mine. His kiss is frantic and his tongue soon pushes against my lips as he begs silently for me to open for him. Which I do. This kiss is nothing like the Jamoca Almond Fudge kiss. Oh, no. I feel warm and it's not from the light desk. I'd like to kiss Snack like this forever. Any anger I was feeling is long gone and in its place, panting want, guttural moans of pleasure and supremely wet panties. The kiss goes on and on. Snack eventually breaks it and ends with another soft sweet kiss.

"What..." I ask breathlessly, "... is going on? What are

you…we… doing?" *He has a girlfriend. A very popular girlfriend who is probably being crowned homecoming queen as we speak. She would kill him if she knew. I'd have to live out my high school career as the nerdy slut that hit on her guy. Life at NDGHS would be miserable.*

"Charlotte?" *I say, not even using a full sentence to ask the question. I never have to with Snack. We speak in a kind of "Minnie/Snack" code with each other.*

"It's over. We broke up. We should've long ago."

"What?"

Snack moves in closer if that's possible. "You've been driving me crazy. I miss you, Minnie. I miss hanging out with you. I've been watching you at school. Watching you get along without me. Watching you move forward without me. Like you don't need me anymore." *With each thing he tells me, he touches me somewhere. My hair. My cheek. My hip.*

I exhale with each touch until I'm air starved and dizzy.

His searching eyes never leave mine. Snack waits for my reaction.

"I thought you didn't want me, that you were the one "moving on." *Part of me wants to kiss all his fears away; the other part is incredibly pissed. I shove him away.*

"Are you fucking kidding me with this?" *I stand and push the skirt of my dress down.* "You don't get to say those things. You don't get to make me feel sorry for you and want to kiss you. Snack, you've been ignoring me everyday, all day, for months. Like, ten months. You've left me alone. So very alone. And NOW you're telling me you miss me?" *I'm willing myself not to cry, I'm so angry.*

Snack backs up and gulps a few times. He finally takes his eyes from mine. The glow from the light desk illuminates them and I see they are wet. He looks up and blinks rapidly and a tear runs down his cheek.

Snack wipes away the tear with the heel of his palm, swallows hard, and returns his gaze to me. He strides the few steps toward me with purpose, backing me up against the light desk. Reaching around my body, he switches off the light. We're in complete darkness. Snack takes my arms and I try to pull away, but he doesn't let me. I'm still mad at him for making me think he stopped caring about me. He wraps my arms around his neck. I hold my breath. These are the moments I've dreamed of since we were twelve.

The next kiss I never got. The kiss he kept from me. His arms around me are the sensation I've hoped for, for so long and never thought I'd have. I'm helpless in his embrace and every cell of my body physically responds with happiness, while I struggle with my anger in a mind-body tug-of-war. I finally exhale and to my surprise it comes out as a sob. My vision clouds and tears begin to drip through my lashes.

God dammit, Snack! Why is he doing this to me?

Snack slides his hands around my waist, and soon I'm pressed up completely against him. A Snackenberg hug.

I indelicately wipe my tears on the lapel of his suit jacket.

"Snack, you asshole. Why? Why are you doing this now?"

"Because I've missed you. So, so much," *Snack confesses beautifully,* "You're right. I have been an asshole, but I'm done. I'm done with Charlotte. I'm done with suicide blondes as you call them. I'm done with pretending they're you when I *should've been with you. You're my best friend. My girl." And with that he finds my lips in the dark and kisses me lightly, our lips salty from our mingled tears. The soft, gentle kiss slowly increases in intensity. I push up on my toes to try and get even closer to him.*

My entire body shakes. I don't know if Snack can feel it, but it's from deep down inside. Deep down in the place next to my heart where I keep all the feels I'm too scared to let out for fear they'll run away with me. The last time I let anything out of there was when my mother came back and didn't even acknowledge me when I was little. That time, my subconscious way of dealing with the pain of her abandonment was jumping off the stairs and splitting my lip wide open. It's almost undetectable now, but I still have a scar from it. I hope to God I don't get a scar this time.

Snack and I stand in the dark, holding each other with our foreheads touching. "I always wanted it to be you with me at the dances, but Clip told me no. Not until I knew for sure you were the one. That I was done with any other girl. All other girls. Because you deserved to be someone's one and only. And I knew he was right. I tried to make Charlotte into you. I really thought it might work. I was doing OK, until I realized you didn't have a date, so I convinced Adam to take you."

I laugh in disbelief. "You? You got Adam to take me?"

"Yeah," Snack says. "It's what I do."

I'm completely baffled and really wish the light was on so I could read Snack's expression. "What do you mean, 'It's what I do?'"

"I make sure you have a date… for dances. One that I know

won't touch you or mess with you. Call you after."

I wrench myself away from Snack, march over to the light switch, and flip it on with an agitated flourish. The entire time I'm cursing under my breath. Cursing Snack and Clip and all the stupid boys I've been set up with. The next time I see my brother I'm going to strangle him! I spin back to face Snack and, dammit, he looks contrite… and beautiful. All my anger floats away. I don't get a chance to cuss him out before he tells me all.

"Minnie, I always wanted to go everywhere you. Every dance, I wished I were with you. Nobody else. But I knew I had to commit. I had to choose to be with just you. Clip convinced me it was a bad idea to be with you. That I'd cheat. That I was too young to be serious. That I'd hurt you. And he swore he'd kill me if I hurt you. So, he introduced me to girls that gave it all away, and I, like an idiot thought he was right. I didn't want to hurt you either. I didn't want to risk losing our friendship." Snack is pacing the room and running his hands through his hair repeatedly. "I didn't want you dating anyone else, so I'd get you dates for dances. I just never understood why you didn't have guys after you all the time."

I'm annoyed enough that I want to piss him off a bit. "Oh, I did." I watch Snack's brow come together in a scowl, but it gives me no pleasure. I give up making him mad and confess. "But they weren't who I wanted."

"Who did you want?"

I look everywhere but at him. Honesty is embarrassing. "Come on, don't make me say it."

Once again Snack is in front of me. This time backing me up against the wall of the classroom. He's not touching me, but he's got his arms caging me in. A trap I'm glad to be caught in.

"Say it," he insists.

I finally look him directly in the eyes. "You. OK... You!" I've been denying and holding it in for so long, now that I've told him, I swear my heart just jumped out of my chest and took a lap around the room. I finally told him! I can't take it back. I don't want to take it back. I close my eyes because it's simply too overwhelming to continue to look into his. And so, I wait for his response.

Snack leans in and kisses me deeply again. That's his response. I push myself off the wall and throw my arms around his neck and thrust my hands into the hair on the back of his head. I suck on Snack's lower lip and when our mouths open to each other, each swipe of our tongues, every deep suckle is an apology to each other for time lost.

What a fucking weird night! A wonderful, weird night. Nothing like I expected.

Snack pulls away and, without warning, throws his head back and howls, "Woo-hoo!" He grabs my hand and pulls us through the door of the journalism room and into the hall. To everyone leaving the dance, to nobody at all, to the universe, he yells out, "My girl! Minnie Cooper is my girl!"

Chapter 8
2014 – The Loft

Snack takes my hand and entwines our fingers again. He starts to walk toward the stairs at the back of the café with me in tow. The stairs lead to the office upstairs. Wookiee lets out a sharp bark from the floor as his tiny legs attempt to keep up. Snack scoops him up and brings him to his chest. Wookiee cuddles into Snack and yawns.

"See, even Wookiee is tired… Let's sleep."

I don't even attempt to argue. I'm exhausted.

As we climb the stairs I ask, "How are we going to sleep up here in your dad's office?"

Snack grumbles something unintelligible. If I didn't already know he wasn't a curser, I would've sworn he said, "Fucker." Snack leans against the back wall at the top of the stairs. "It was"—Snack turns back to continue ascending—"until he cheated on my mom and they divorced."

I know this is not a pleasant topic for Snack. After years of marriage, Snack's dad, Robert, had an affair and ran off with one of the vendors for the café—a woman in her twenties. Younger than Snack at the time. The worst part, in my opinion? She looked just like Colette only a newer model. I don't know every detail of the story, but who would leave a woman like Colette? It's like movie stars that fuck around on their gorgeous, talented spouses. To the outsider, it's illogical and greedy and fucking mean.

Snack flips a light switch at the top of the stairs, and I'm surprised at what I see or don't see. Gone is Snack's dad's cramped paper strewn office with its beat-up couch and old gray office desk. Gone are the stacks of paper goods and ceramic mugs. It's all been replaced and remodeled into a gorgeous, expansive loft apartment. If I were guessing, I'd say it mimics the footprint of the café downstairs, which is not tiny, for square footage.

"My mom was going to move in here. She said after my dad was gone and I was married and rarely home, the house felt too large and ridiculous."

"This is amazing!" I spin in place to appreciate every detail: the solid wood wainscoting, the multihued wall finish, the subtle lighting. Each aspect has been thoughtfully planned.

The ceiling is high and vaulted. It's one large space. A large open kitchen with warm cherry cabinets, stainless steel appliances, and black granite counters is a chef's dream. The large kitchen island merges into the open living space, which has a big inviting chestnut leather couch, a couple of chairs, and a coffee/ottoman thing—I never know what to call that particular piece of furniture. A floor to ceiling window takes up the front of the loft. The streetlights from below illuminate the falling snow outside. Some of it sticks to the top part of the window.

I just walk around in awe. "Wow! Snack this is so great"

There's a screened off area to the right. I peek around the screen and view a king-size bed. I immediately wish I could climb in and crash.

"That's the bedroom." Snack lifts an eyebrow and gestures with a Vanna White worthy flourish.

"Really?" I ask with equal sarcasm. "Thanks for elaborating, that would've escaped me."

Snack laughs, nuzzling Wookiee. "Nothing gets by her, huh, Wookiee? Smart cookie, that one."

Snack points out the large bathroom adjacent to the bedroom space and the walk-in closet.

I'd picked up a stray newspaper from the café on the way up. Wookiee hasn't gone potty since we got on the train, but I know he won't step foot out in this snowstorm. I explain the situation to Snack as I pop into the attached bathroom and lay a thick layer of paper in a corner.

I point to the newspaper as I walk out of the bathroom. "Sorry about that."

"Well, a man's gotta have a place to go." Snack kisses Wookiee on the snout and places him gently on the floor. "Right, buddy." My heart puddles on the floor. Snack is being affectionate with Wook and Wook is letting him. Why can't it be that way with Henry? Henry. I admit to myself, I haven't thought about him much since I got back to Downers Grove.

I shiver. This loft is beautiful, but cold. Not cold as in uninviting, but really freezing cold. My brain pushes my manners aside and I bark out, "Fuck, it's fucking cold up here."

Snack snorts. "Never one to underuse the fuck word, huh, Min."

It's my turn to laugh. Snack just alluded to an old Cooper family joke.

I stand outside the bathroom door, screaming at my little brother once again. "Sid, jeez, get out of the fucking bathroom. I need to get ready for school. Snack's waiting."

"Wilhelmina Jane, don't say the fuck word!" Dad yells from down the hall as he comes toward me.

"You mean, don't say the F-word, don't you, Dad?"

"Fuck! Yes! I mean don't use the F-word. It doesn't sound nice."

Dad and I smile to stifle our mutual laughs, but they quickly overcome us.

Dad winks at me and bangs on the bathroom door. "Sid, get out of the fucking bathroom! Your sister needs to do her fucking girl stuff."

"Nice use of the fuck word, Dad."

"That's enough out of you, Min."

Snack's next words shake me from my memory.

"You're right. It's pretty darn cold up here."

Pretty darn cold? What is he? A monk? It is sort of adorable that he isn't naturally profane. Unlike me.

Snack moves toward the large stone fireplace that wraps around the angled wall from the living space, so it's also partially in the bedroom space. "I'll start a fire. You want to turn up the thermostat? It's on the wall near the top of the stairs."

I go over and push the heat level up. Still shivering, I cross my arms and rub my hands up and down them. I stomp my feet, too.

Snack squats and places a couple of logs in the fireplace. He turns and smiles at me. "Frozen?"

"Almost." I respond through nearly chattering teeth.

"We don't run the heat up here all the time since there isn't anyone up here all day." Snack lights a match and tosses it under the balled-up newspaper. Of course, it lights right away. It's Snack. Perfect, Eagle-fucking-Scout Snack.

I watch his shoulders and back move as he attends to the area around the hearth. I know what's under that gray sweater. Snack's muscular torso. Just imagining it makes me exhale quietly to myself. I scold myself yet again for thinking about him like that when I know he's still grieving his wife.

Snack stands, wipes his hands of his chore with satisfaction, and then turns and strides over to me. He stands about one foot away. "Get in bed."

What? I feel my entire body flush. Get in bed? With Snack?

My expression must telegraph my confusion—if not my delight at his order—because Snack chuckles. "Yes, take your shoes off, but leave your clothes on and get in bed. You'll be warmer. And I know you're tired."

Wookiee wastes no time following Snack's orders. He has already made his way up onto the bed and barks his agreement with Snack's idea. I'm being herded.

Snack pokes the fire a few more times. Once in bed, I roll over to watch Snack's back some more. What's wrong with me? Why can't I stop myself from these thoughts? He bows his head and lets out a long deep sigh.

Wookiee comes to roll up in a cinnamon bun shape in front of me, but not before he barks at Snack to stop what he's doing.

Snack looks over his shoulder at both of us. One of his eyebrows raises and the same corner of his lip curls up in amusement. "OK, buddy, I'm coming. Wow! He's a bossy little thing, Min."

"Yep, he keeps me in line."

Snack crosses to the other side of the bed behind me. Two loud thumps tell me he's taken off his shoes. I don't move a muscle. This is really happening. He's getting in the bed! A gush of cold air blows over me when he raises the sheet and duvet to slip in. I shudder.

"You're cold. Come here." With a quick move of his powerful arm, he pulls my back tight against his chest. "Let's spoon. You'll be warmer."

I can't or don't argue.

Wookiee readjusts so he's even closer to me, his head propped on my neck. He has to be staring right at Snack.

My suspicion is confirmed when Snack says, "Hello, Buddy!" I hear him kiss Wookiee on the head and am momentarily jealous until I feel his breath in my hair.

Everything in me tells me to scoot back a little into his embrace. I want to be close to him, I've always wanted to be close to him my whole life, but I'm pretty sure he's just looking for comfort from an old friend, not a hookup. Instead, I position myself into my usual sleep position. I lift my lower leg up toward my chest.

Snack laughs in my ear. "You were always terrible at this."

I peek back at him. "What? Spooning? I'm excellent at spooning."

"No, you're not. You sleep like a can opener. It's like trying to spoon in the cooking utensil drawer."

He's actually right and I chuckle. I've never been too good at this. Reaching behind me, I smack him on the butt or hip or something, I can't really tell, I just know it was firm. Snack pulls me in closer.

Then I hear him sniffle and something drips on my ear. Is he crying? Yes, he is. His emotions must be all over the place. I can feel his chest vibrating, heaving against my back. He squeezes me tighter. What should I do? What should I say? Without warning, my own tears come softly at first and then in gushing waves. We hold each other and cry for what seems like hours. I don't really know precisely what we're crying about, but the emotion in the room alone is palpable. The source of this shared sadness could be, oh-so-many things: the death of his wife, Megan, our always off-track love, his now motherless children, my overwhelming loneliness and pathetic "relationship" with Henry, seeing each other after such a long time, or even, in my case, at least, guilt over being attracted to a newly widowed man.

I can't take this much longer. I slam the floodgates shut

and turn my head toward him to meet his eyes. I sniffle back as much emotion as I can. "That blubbering is truly unsexy. You may never get laid again if you do that in front of girls."

Snack's face breaks into a huge grin, and for the first time all night I hear his carefree laugh that I missed for so long.

"Minnie, I've really missed you. You have no idea."

I finally admit aloud to him and myself that I felt the same. "I've missed you, too, Snack."

Snack blows out a cleansing sigh and pulls me back against him, wrapping me tighter in his arms. "OK, Can opener, we'll talk about it tomorrow. Now, go to sleep."

Chapter 9
1999 – So Very Happy, So Very Sad

I'm the happiest I've ever been. Like ever, ever.

Snack brought me home after the homecoming dance last night and kissed me at the door like a real date. Getting my brain to shut off and go to sleep was a real challenge. I eventually succumbed sometime after one thirty in the morning. That was the last time I looked at the clock.

Snack showed up at my house at seven thirty this morning. I was just coming out of an amazing dream about him when it's cut short by Sid's cracking adolescent screech. "Minnie, Snack's here! I'm sending him up to your room!"

"No!" I yell through my bedroom door. Suddenly, I don't want Snack to see me with bedhead and morning breath.

I jump up from my bed and scramble to find my favorite gray Stormtrooper sweatshirt. It's somewhere on the floor in the pile of clothes that aren't quite dirty enough to put down the laundry chute. After digging halfway through the pile, I find it. After pulling it on over my tank top, I move over to my dresser, grab a hair tie and scoop my unruly brown mop up into a high pony. OK, just need to brush my teeth and I'll be presentable...

"Hey, there's my girl." I practically jump a foot. I didn't even hear my door open. Snack's in my room. This shouldn't be surprising. He's always been welcome, but for some reason it's different this morning. "Why did you tell Sid I couldn't come up?"

An awkward shyness overcomes me, and I pull at the bottom of my oversized sweatshirt, trying to cover my boxer shorts. I've never felt exposed in front of Snack before. Hell, he's seen me in my swimsuit. What's my deal?

"I was still in bed. I wanted to get dressed before you saw me."

Snack lowers his head and tilts it to the side. He presses his lips together, but a slow smirk turns up the corners of his mouth. He looks at my bare feet and his gaze wanders up my naked legs. His hooded eyes finally meet mine. "Oh man, I wish I'd gotten up here a minute earlier... I'm sorry I missed that."

Swoon.

Snack plops down on the bed next to where I'm standing. Reaching out for my boxers, he takes the hem between his thumb and forefinger and tugs it lightly. The back of his finger grazes my upper thigh, leaving tingly warmth in its wake. "Nice boxers," he says. "Whose are they?"

I have no idea. Probably my dad's or Clip's. I shrug.

"I'll bring you some of mine. I only want you wearing mine from now on."

"Uh, O-Kay." I stutter in response to his demand and most definitely his touch. I have no problem with that. Must be

another one of Snack's weird possessive things.

Snack twists the fabric of my boxers around his fingers and pulls me toward him. "Come here and kiss me. I can't believe you haven't kissed me yet."

My heart thumps out of control and my brain is frozen. I've heard actors say things like that in movies, but in real life? I guess it does actually happen. I want nothing more than to push him back on my bed and kiss him until lunchtime, but I haven't peed or brushed my teeth or anything yet.

Untangling his fingers from my boxers after much resistance from Snack, I back away toward the door. Everything in me wants to travel in the opposite direction—toward him, not away, but physiology wins out. That and fresh breath.

"I just need to run and do a couple of things," I say and then add formally, "Make yourself at home."

Snack laughs. "I always do."

I sprint to the bathroom to pee and brush my teeth.

When I return, Snack is sitting cross-legged on my bed. He's made himself comfortable just as I suggested. There's a tray in the middle of my comforter with a sumptuous breakfast of orange juice and chocolate chip Eggos drenched in butter and maple syrup.

"Hi!" he says.

"Hi!" I reply more comfortable now that I've used the bathroom.

"I brought you breakfast."

"I see. Very fancy. I didn't know you knew how to cook… or toast," I add as I pick up an Eggo.

Snack leans forward and takes a bite of the Eggo, his lips swiping across my fingers as they retreat. He licks some of the buttery syrup left behind off his lips.

Zing! My heart takes over. I toss the Eggo back on the tray and launch myself onto Snack. I can't kiss him fast enough. I push him back on my Star Wars pillows, amused that his face is right next to the one of Han Solo printed on my pillowcase. Nerd girl nirvana. Snack kisses me back with a kind of passionate enthusiasm I've only read about.

He softly kisses my upper lip and then traps my lower lip between his teeth in a soft bite. Soon his tongue is moving languidly over mine.

Every neuron in my lips, my mouth, and my body is firing. There is a warmth pooling low in my abdomen. I arch my body into his and slide my leg up one of his. The roughness of his jeans against my bare legs arouses me further, causing the fine hairs on my entire body to stand up. Snack slips his hand under my sweatshirt and tank top to my lower back. I'm keenly aware of his pinkie touching the edge of the waistband of my boxers. Somewhere on the periphery of my awareness I hear the phone ringing. It's beyond easy to ignore considering my current situation.

Loud knocks on my bedroom door startle us, and Snack and I jump to the edge of the bed.

I quickly straighten any dishevelment of my clothes and then yell, "Come in!"

The latch unclicks and the door to my bedroom swings open. My dad is standing in the doorway with an undecipherable look on his face.

"Snack," he intones flatly. "I didn't know you were here."

I can't tell what Dad is thinking. Mad? Upset? Are we going to be in trouble for being alone together in my room? It's not like it's so unusual. I mean, sure, every time before it was just hanging out, not making out, but still.

My dad takes a seat on the bed next to me.

I'm uncomfortable, so much so that my skin crawls and I shudder. Snack and I were just making out in this very spot. I'm working hard to control my breathing. I don't know about Snack, but it's not easy to slam on the brakes that quickly.

My dad puts his arm around me and tells me to hold Snack's hand. "Guys, I don't know how to tell you this, but I just got a phone call from your mom, Snack. Charlotte Carpenter's parents have been looking for you." My dad squeezes his arm around me tighter.

"Why?" Snack asks, his voice thin and confused.

"Charlotte didn't come home last night."

"What?" Snack twists his body to look at my father and me. "She went home with Adam. I saw them leave together."

My dad continues to look at the floor, not us. "Yeah... um, Adam and Charlotte were in a bad wreck. Evidently, they decided to go driving around after homecoming... Snack weren't you supposed to drive Charlotte home?"

"Yes, Gil, sir, yes, I was, but we broke up at the dance... and then I went and found Minnie with Adam... Is? Are they all right?" Snack's eyes widen and the color drains from his face.

My dad sighs. "No, they're not. Evidently, Adam lost control of the car... probably speeding. Charlotte wasn't wearing a seatbelt."

I can't stop my entire body from shaking, even though my

dad is holding me firmly.

Snack interjects with a thick mumble. "She doesn't like them."

"They went off the road and down an embankment," Dad continues. "Adam has a broken arm and both his legs are damaged. Charlotte was more seriously injured."

"She's alive, isn't she?" My words tremble.

"Yes," my dad replies quietly, but not hopefully.

"This is all my fault!" Snack stands quickly from the bed and goes to the door of my room. "I need to go over to the Carpenter's."

My dad gets up and goes to him. "They're at the hospital with Charlotte. She was airlifted to Children's Memorial in the city."

Snack breaks down in huge gulping sobs that rock his whole body. Then out of nowhere he slams his fist into my bedroom door. When he pulls his hand back, it's scraped and bloody. My father grabs him and holds him, whispering something to him.

I do nothing. I don't know what to do. I just stare at the scene in front of me. How could I possibly be so happy one minute and paralyzed with fear and sadness the next?

I barely register when Snack and my dad leave, other than Dad kissing me on the top of my head. I vaguely recall nodding when Dad asked me to stay at home with Sid.

I started the day the happiest I've ever been. And now, I'm alone and scared.

Well, not completely alone, because I can hear Sid blasting Mario Kart in the other room. Even though he pisses me off most of the time, I suddenly miss Clip and wish he wasn't away at college.

When the tears come, they gush from between my lashes. I don't exactly know who or what they are for. Charlotte? Snack? Me? Sounds I've never heard before come out of me. Thankfully, Sid's game is loud enough that he doesn't notice.

Chapter 10
2014 – Morning After in the Loft

Soft licking on my bare shoulder wakes me. My brain races to keep up with the rate my body is waking up. Where am I? Oh, that's right. The loft above SNACKS. And I'm in bed… with Snack. I slept so deeply once I let my tiredness overtake me, like sleeping next to Snack was the safest most natural place for me to be.

Lick. Lick. As much as I wish the licking was Snack, it isn't. I know only too well, it's Wookiee. Licking me on the face, neck, or shoulder is his way of waking me up in the early morning to go out. The strange thing about this is, he's snuggled *behind* my shoulder, licking it. Which means he's sleeping *between* Snack and me. Wook never, ever wants to sleep between Henry and me. He sleeps on the furthest corner of the bed away from us and only comes up to the top of the bed in the morning to wake me. Only if Henry is out of town will Wookiee cuddle down next to me in bed. Maybe Wookiee can sense something I haven't allowed myself to fully acknowledge yet. Maybe Henry isn't the one for us. For me. I've heard animals are perceptive like that. It just figures Wookiee has snuggled up to Snack. It seems even tiny purse dogs, male ones at that, are attracted to Snack.

I turn to pet Wookiee and stop the cleansing of my shoulder. Behind Wookiee's cute face is another one. Snack's. He's still dead to the world. He finally looks unworried and less tired. Gorgeous boy. His blond hair and beard gleam under the rays of moonlight streaming through the cracks in the blinds. The corners of his lips are turned up. I wonder what he's dreaming of.

Looking a little more closely, I see that Snack is no longer wearing the thermal he had on when he came to bed after taking off his sweater. I, too, only have on my tank top and boy shorts. The memory of feeling too warm in the middle of the night and pulling my top and leggings off and throwing them from the bed returns. I guess we were both exhausted, because neither of us seemed to have awakened and acknowledged the other stripping. Too bad! Jesus, Min, what are you doing? The man is in mourning, grieving his dead wife, the mother of his children, and you're bemoaning the fact that you didn't have a midnight hookup!

Wook nudges me insistently with his cold, wet nose. There is no escaping it. I have to get up and walk the furball. I roll to the edge of the bed, sit up, and grab a glass of water that Snack must have placed on the bedside table at some point last night. The water is cool and alerting. I rub my eyes a couple of times and stand up. Wookiee stretches and pads over to me, strutting across the duvet when I pat my thigh to tell him it's time to get up and go out to do his business. Hopefully the snow has stopped falling, so he won't have to resort to the newspaper. I softly shush him, knowing he occasionally barks when he wants me to move faster. I don't want him to wake Snack.

Through the large, arched window in the kitchen/dining area, I see nothing but white. I scoop up Wookiee and walk over to look out. Downtown Downers Grove looks as if it's been under assault by the Stay Puft Marshmallow Man. Even as dark as it still is outside, I can see it's a white, puffy marshmallow world of new fallen snow reflecting the dwindling moonlight. Apparently, I've awoken on the ice planet Hoth. It's very quiet. I can't hear any cars or people. When I glance at the clock in the kitchen, it tells me it's 5:37. About Wookiee's usual wake-up time. The usual early morning coffee drinkers probably won't be in anytime soon since the city snowplows, apparently, haven't even come through.

I whisper to Wookiee, "Come on. Let's go out." I place him on the floor and he skitters over to the chair where my purse is. He knows his leash is in there. I dig it out and snap it on him. Then I dress him in his red and black buffalo check winter jacket. I smirk while putting his jacket on, knowing this walk will be extremely brief, if it can even be considered a walk at all.

I snatch my jeans up from beside the bed and pull them on, pluck Snack's large sweater from the floor, throw it over my head, and shove my feet into my boots. Picking Wookiee up, we tiptoe down the stairs and go to the front door.

Fortunately, Snack only set the deadlock, so I don't need a key to open it. There's about two feet right in front of the building that is untouched by the massive snowdrifts left from the storm thanks to the awning over the front entrance. I place Wookiee on the ground and he does his business.

"Good boy, Wookiee. What a good boy. Now, come on, let's go in"

Wookiee doesn't move.

"Wookiee, come on! I'm cold. *You're* cold. Let's go!

He looks up at me with wide eyes and stands there shivering, then barks a piercing, demanding bark. He wants me to come get him. Dammit! I really didn't want to have to walk out of the doorway. It's fucking colder than a Tauntaun's left nut out here. I give into the tiny monarch's command and walk the two feet to pick him up. When I turn to walk back into the café, a sudden gust of icy wind cause the door to slam and I'm suddenly covered in an ice-cold wet blanket.

"FUCK!" I think and then immediately say aloud. Looking up, I see the force of the door slam triggered a pile of snow to cut loose from the awning and land on me.

"Well, shit!" I shake off as much as I can, but some of it's down the back of the sweater.

Quickly, with Wookiee under my arm, I rush back into the café. Setting him down to the floor carefully, but firmly, I shake my finger at him. "Dammit, dog. You couldn't walk back in? I had to come get you?" Unmoved my by admonition, Wookiee shakes off any wetness that fell on him. I do the same. I need to get out of these damp clothes and get warm.

Tiptoeing back up to the loft, I take the dog's coat and leash off. His feet are wet and so are my hair, neck, and back. I need a towel. It's still pretty dark up here, and I move gingerly so I won't crash into anything and wake Snack.

Suddenly, a light pops on. I jump and grab my chest, pulling my damp Yorkie closer. Some sort of unintelligible scream escapes my lips.

Snack is propped up on a bunch of pillows in the bed, the soft glow of the bedside lamp casting shadows on all the beautiful bulges and valleys of his undressed upper body. He must have taken off the thermal while I was out with Wookiee. In a word: He looks edible.

I consciously acknowledge that I'm number one, speechless. And number two, filled with unbridled hunger. A not unpleasant heat floods my core. I audibly exhale.

"What happened to you?" Snack chuckles and points to my hair.

I must look a mess. All my desire leaves me muddled, and I trip and stutter as I tell him about Wookiee not coming in and being accosted by a blob of snow. I pull Snack's sweater off and survey it for damage. It doesn't look too wet. I hang it over a chair to dry.

When I look back up at Snack, I'm taken aback by his change of mood. His smile vanishes and his eyes grow dark and heavy. He shifts slightly in bed and lets his gaze move all over my body. The remaining clothes I have on, my tank top and skinny jeans, don't leave much to the imagination. His stare makes me feel even more naked.

Snack pulls back the duvet on the side of the bed I was

sleeping in and pats the mattress. "You need to get warm. Get in bed." Snack's voice is low and serious.

Get in bed. The same words he said last night. Somehow, I don't think they mean quite the same thing this morning. Everything in me wants to rush over and slide between the sheets. The magnetic tug toward him is strong.

"Uh-OK." Again, I stumble over my words. "I, uh, I'm just gonna wipe Wookiee's feet and towel off my hair." I point over my shoulder and then spin in place to march into the bathroom. "Be right back."

"Don't be too long," Snack yells as I shut the door.

Oh. My. God. What's happening? Is something going to happen or does he just want to talk. Am I just imagining the way he looked over my body? I think I want something to happen. Is that OK, considering what Snack's been going through? I peel off my soggy jeans, robotically towel off my hair and wipe the areas of my body that are wet. I dry Wook's paws as best I can. Taking a look in the mirror, I wipe the mascara smudges from under my eyes. Pee! I should pee. I do it quickly and then stand to wash my hands. While doing so I look up in the mirror again and smack my lips. Dry mouth. Probably morning breath, too. Opening the medicine cabinet, I survey it for toothpaste and find some in no time. I also see two toothbrushes, but I don't know whose they are, so I just squeeze out a bit of paste and scrub it on my teeth with my finger and then swish it around. After spitting, I look in the mirror again. I catch myself breathing in low pants. I realize I'm taking my time because of the uncertainty of what will happen when I walk out of the bathroom.

Snack yells through the door, concern in his voice. "Are you OK?"

"Uh, yeah, coming!" Saying that sort of makes me laugh. Because I *am* practically coming. All it took was a few glances and darkly intoned words from Snack to get me there. I think I'm in trouble. Potentially good trouble, but trouble.

I scoop Wookiee up and open the bathroom door. I'm almost afraid to make eye contact with Snack for fear I'll combust before I get near him. Sort of tossing Wook onto the duvet, I slide in between the sheets, backside first, but not before sneaking a look at Snack. He's visually tracking my every move. Once I'm in bed, I'm instantly pulled backward into Snack's embrace.

"You're cold." Snack huffs into my hair near my ear.

"You're not." I gulp. He isn't. Snack is warm, hot even. His arms hug around my waist and his hands move up and graze the bottom of my breasts. I arch my back at the sensation his touch evokes. My nipples peak and harden almost painfully. He cups my breasts in his large warm, hands. His thumbs scrape deliciously across my aroused nipples, causing even more swirling pooling desire in my core.

Reaching back I run my hand down the curve of Snack's ass and across his upper thigh. Grasping it, I encourage him to throw it over my legs and in doing so am happily surprised to feel his hard erection at my lower back.

"Is this OK?" Snack's breath is hot in my ear.

I want to say, "More than OK." But I answer by spinning to face him and reaching up to hold his delectably scruffy jawline in my hands.

"You tell me. I don't want to do anything that we'll regret."

"I know, I've been thinking the same thing, but I just want to feel something again. Something other than sadness. Is that OK?"

I open my mouth to answer but evidently my eyes have already given permission.

He kisses me. This is not sweet, delicate kissing. This is full-on desperate-to-feel desire. We hungrily devour each other's lips and tongues. We nip and lick and bite as if we'd never tasted another human before. I remember kissing Snack in the past but not with this ferocity—this level of need. Our bodies imitate our mouths; we can't get enough of the other. Snack's hands are in my hair, then running down my arms, then on my breasts again. I push myself against his considerable hardness with slow, sliding thrusts. Snack ducks his head and sucks on my shoulder. I throw my head back to give him more access and, as I do, he leaves my collarbone, pushing the straps of my tank top down and revealing my chest, to bring his hot, wet mouth onto one of my nipples. Humming, he sucks it in deeply, rolling his tongue around it. My clit throbs in response and our slow thrusts accelerate to rhythmic rocking. The fabric of my boy shorts and his boxer briefs combine to amp up the level of friction. I slide my hand into his boxers and stroke the plush firmness of the head of his cock with my fingertips. Snack groans and pushes himself into my hand.

Through our haze of lust, Wookiee starts bounding

around at the foot of the bed and barking frantically. Noise from downstairs becomes louder as we hear someone moving around in the café.

"Daddy!" A child yells up the stairs. Oh, crap! It's Fifi! She opens the door and looks for her daddy. That means Aiden and probably Gil and Colette are down there, too. Never thought to lock the door.

Snack and I freeze. We are so busted. My hand on his junk. His mouth on my breast. We pull away, look at each other wide-eyed and begin laughing conspiratorially. Snack places a hand over my mouth and a snort escapes my nose.

Snack hollers from over his shoulder with a cajoling singsong voice. "Hey, Fifi, Daddy's not dressed yet. Stay down there with Grandma. OK?"

"OK, Daddy!" she shouts and the door closes.

I sigh deeply and groan with frustration. If Fifi hadn't interrupted, Snack would be deep inside me by now.

Snack obviously feels the same way. When I try to pull my hand off him he grabs it and growls. "This will be continued. You know what? I'm taking you out tonight. On a *real* date with no kids or parents for miles. Understood?"

I nod and smile. Then Snack kisses me with one of the light, sweet kisses we never got to earlier. Sadly, he rolls out of the bed and stands with his back at a three quarter angle to me He looks down at his cock and shakes his head. I agree, it's a waste. He looks over his shoulder and blows me a kiss. I blow one back. Pulling on his jeans, thermal and sweater while walking around the room, he readies himself to start his day.

I'm in contrast, languishing half-naked in bed.

"Aren't you getting up?"

"No, I'm not. I'm too frustrated." I whine. Then before I can check myself I add, "It's too bad those toothbrushes in there aren't electric."

Snack laughs. "No! No toothbrush." Snack crawls back over and kisses me slowly and sweetly. "And stay away from the shower massage, too. Just hold on to all of that until tonight. I'll make it worth the wait, I promise."

"OK, no toothbrush." I draw an X across my chest with my finger. "I promise, too."

Snack leaps off the bed. I toss a pillow at him, which he catches with one hand and hurls back at me. I grab it, hold it over my mouth, and yell all my sexual frustration into it. When I emerge from my scream fest, I spy Snack holding Wookiee and heading downstairs.

"Just get up, get dressed, and come down for breakfast."

I moan again.

"I'll know what you're doing if I have to wait longer than five minutes for you to come down. Don't think I don't. No. Shower. Massage."

"OK, OK."

I mentally calculate how many hours I have to wait until our "date."

Chapter 11
2000 – Never Ready for This

Charlotte died three days after homecoming.

I'm new to this. All of this. Overwhelming infatuation. Unexpected death. I don't think at age eighteen these are supposed to be feelings I'm comfortable with. Really, when you get right down to it, are you supposed to be comfortable falling in love? I mean the first part of that phrase is falling— and falling sucks. And death—I hope nobody ever becomes comfortable with that. My Mimi talked about funerals she'd attended and death all the time. Maybe you do get comfortable. Or maybe it gets easier to talk about and your throat doesn't swell up and you don't choke on your words anymore.

Charlotte died three days after homecoming.

When my dad and Colette took him to see Charlotte, Snack was allowed into the ICU at the Children's Hospital. He told me she was unrecognizable, swollen, hair shaved off, tubes going in and out of her body and one down her throat connected to a breathing machine. He said he talked to her and held her hand, but he knew she wasn't really there. He couldn't feel her there. When he left the room, he vomited in a trashcan outside. He was most surprised that Charlotte's parents came out and hugged him. After he failed to take care of her and get her home safely, they were comforting him. Mr. and Mrs. Carpenter told him they knew how willful Charlotte was. They also knew she and Snack had broken up and she was getting a ride home with Adam. By some miracle, she'd called to tell them right before she left the dance. It was little consolation, but Snack said it made him feel less guilty. He could only imagine how Adam was doing.

Quietly, with no announcement or warning, Charlotte's family decided to withdraw life support after the doctors told her the brain scan was not reassuring and she probably had no chance of regaining any sort of life. She would be on a ventilator the rest of her life. She would be fed with a tube the rest of her life. She wouldn't walk or tell them she loved them ever again. So they did the least selfish thing parents could do. They let her go.

Adam didn't return to school for the end of his senior year. He had months of rehab and homeschooling and still wasn't sure if he'd be in any shape to start college in the fall. Snack and I visited him a couple of times. We never mentioned Charlotte. Neither did he.

***

If Snack and I were tight before, we were inseparable after Charlotte's death. It was probably more like hiding out. We turned into each other and shut the rest of the world out.

Charlotte's funeral was a week to the day after homecoming. Adam couldn't go because he was still in the hospital. I heard Charlotte's family went to see him to tell him she died. I couldn't even imagine his anguish. When my overly active brain started to fabricate a movie of what is was probably like, I mentally shoved it away. It was hard enough watching Snack struggle right in front of me.

Snack and I, without ever having a discussion, never touch each other in front of anyone—at school, in public, especially at Charlotte's funeral. That is really hard. I want nothing more than to hold his hand. It has to wait until we get into the car. Then I hold his hand for an hour and tell him repeatedly that what happened to Charlotte and Adam isn't his fault. He finally points to his head and says, "This knows"—he holds his free hand over his heart—"but this doesn't."

I take his hand, the one on his chest, and kiss the palm. "I don't know anything about death, but I know about loss." My mother, my sick lost-to-me mother had been in my thoughts during the past week, a lot. "It's going to get better. It's never going to be the same, but it will get better." Then I lean over and kiss his chest, right over his heart.

Snack reaches up and runs his hands through my hair and then down to my cheek. He tilts my face up to look at me. "All I want to do right now is go home and lie on the couch in the family room with you. And kiss you. It might be wrong, but it's all I want."

"I don't think it's wrong, Snack, but maybe because that's all I want to do, too."

This was our answer to the sadness and guilt about being together in the wake of the tragedy of Charlotte's death. Turn to each other.

At first we kept our relationship quiet. Not an easy feat after Snack loudly announced to the student body at homecoming that I was his girl, but it didn't seem right to flaunt our burgeoning relationship in front of the world. The death of Charlotte Carpenter belonged to the whole school and the whole town of Downers Grove. A beautiful, brilliant girl—gone. It wouldn't be out of the cycle of town chatter for quite a while. Certainly, not this school year. As editor of the yearbook, I immediately got the staff working on a tribute to Charlotte as a late addition. It didn't escape me how hypocritical that was. She was dead. I was the one alive and dating her ex-boyfriend. I was reaping the rewards of this awful tragedy. Although, no one ever said it aloud, I was thinking it, so logically the rest of the world was, too.

I must correct myself: No one ever said it aloud except Lorna D'Innocenzio. Funny name for the least innocent girl I knew. Lorna had been a pain in my ass since second grade. She made fun of me. Teased me. Routinely called me "Fugly Mouse." She did anything and everything to get Snack's attention at the bus stop when we were kids. She even went so far as to flash her naked boobs at him—once she had them, which was pretty early, like fifth grade or something. She was a really pretty girl with a really ugly soul. I knew it then. It was solidified when she cornered me in the first floor girls' bathroom.

"Fugly, you must be completely fucking stupid. And

heartless. Really? Do you really think Snackenberg is for you? He was Charlotte's. They were perfect and gorgeous together. Then you come along and break them up, and she's suddenly dead! It's a little weird, you know. Nobody. I mean NO-BO-DY is going to accept you two being together."

By this time, her sneering ugly-beautiful face is right up in mine. Any closer and we'd be kissing. I have no defense, physically or verbally. She's only saying things I've already said to myself.

The only thing that saves me is the bang of the girl's bathroom door hitting the wall.

I've never been happy to see cheerleaders in my life, but when a herd of them barrel into the bathroom, Lorna backs away from me, moves over to a mirror, and pretends like she's fixing her hair. I take the opportunity to slide against the wall past the cheerleaders.

One of them, Megan, who's always been nice to me, catches my attention before I creep out. "Minnie, you OK?" I didn't even know she knew my name.

"Yes." I sniffle, not looking at her. As I exit, I hear a swell of noise. Loud yelling. Something like "D'Innocenzio, you bitch" or something like that. I'll forever be grateful to Megan for defending me like that.

Staring at the floor in the hallway and processing what just happened, a tear falls from my eye and splashes on the linoleum. When I finally look up and down the hall, all I see is Snack, standing at his locker and staring at me intently. The hallway is full of between-class traffic, but it all falls away when I see him. We might as well be the only two people in the school.

100

He kicks his locker shut when I approach him. Without words, he pulls me into his arms right up against his chest. I guess the not touching in public charade is over. Snack asks me what happened, and I blubber the goings on that just occurred in the bathroom with Lorna and Megan.

Snack tips my head up and fixes me with his Siberian Husky eyes. "Forget her! Never mind anything Lorna said. Nobody knows what's happening with two people except those two people. She doesn't know anything about Charlotte and me or you and me for that matter." I swallow back my tears and nod. We walk with Snack's arm around me, cupping my hip. Snack just announced, again, to the whole school that we're a couple.

Snack and I spend every possible moment together. Days at school. Evenings in his downstairs family room or at my house. I suspect my dad really might give us trouble about being alone in my room without the door open. I prefer the nights at Snack's house. Colette and Mr. Snackenberg at the shop. The whole house to ourselves.

I don't know how I got my dad to agree to let me hang out over at Snack's unsupervised. Maybe it was because he didn't want me moping around, thinking about Charlotte and Adam, and the residual guilt that went, sadly, along with being with Snack. Or maybe it's because I flat out told him Snack and I weren't having sex and wouldn't be having sex until we were twenty-three because that's when we would be well out of college, and we couldn't fuck up our lives, of course.

Not that I didn't want to.

I did.

We came close one time, but Snack stopped us from going too far.

"Don't, don't you want to?"

"Minnie, when I'm finally with you—inside you, I know, for me, it will be perfect. I just want to make sure it's perfect for you, too. Not just some random Wednesday when you come over after LARPing Club in that sexy Robin Hood costume."

I smack Snack lightly on the chest and he grabs my hand. "It's not Robin Hood. It's Link from Legend of Zelda and you know that."

"Honestly, I wouldn't care if you were dressed as a Mario brother, but you might have a few regrets, if your first time was on the 80s plush carpet of my parent's family room and dressed as Peter Pan."

"Link!"

"Whatever."

It didn't matter what I wore or where we were or what fucking night of the week it was, I knew it would be perfect with Snack. But it didn't happen that night or at all because even though Snack had had sex before with other girls, for noble reasons he didn't with me.

Just because we weren't having actual naked sex didn't mean we weren't fooling around and having SWCO: Sex With your Clothes On. We had lots of SWCO!

"Aaah, Oh, oh, oh my God, Min—nie!" Snack yelled while grabbing my hips as I rocked into his hardness and he thrust against my shorts.

"Mmm," I hum with satisfaction. I loved to make him scream to the heavens and me when he let loose. I loved the way his head fell back on the couch cushion as I straddled him, partially clothed mind you, on the floor with his back against

the couch. I loved the way he would look up at me afterward with complete relaxation in his face.

Snack leans up and kisses me, licking the sheen of perspiration from my upper lip. "I love your sounds."

"I was just thinking the same thing about yours," I whisper into his cheek.

Snack lifts me gently and sits me on the floor next to him. I adjust my underwear through my pants.

Snack takes my chin and turns my face to him, his eyes burn into mine. "How wet are you?"

"Soaked," I reply, dropping my eyes, embarrassed by my own horniness. His low tone and candor only make me want him more.

"Good! Me, too." Snack's gaze moves toward the crotch of his track pants. There's a large wet spot there.

I giggle. "Was that me or you?"

"Some of you, and a whole lot of me." Snack chuckles and stands. "I'm gonna go upstairs and change… again. You're gonna wear me out, Min!"

"Sorry," I chirp as I move up to sit on the couch.

Snack leans down and kisses me on the forehead and then the nose. "Oh, never be sorry for that Minnie. Never be sorry for making me—"

"Come?"

"I was going to say happy but come works, too. How about you?"

I smile. "You always make me 'happy.'"

I'm not lying he does. Every single time.

Chapter 12
2014 – Dad

Snack and I couldn't have been any more fucking obvious the morning after we spent the night in the loft. He came downstairs in the clothes he had on the night before with my dog tucked under his arm. I appeared five minutes later in a new change of clothes but the most appalling rat's nest of a head of hair. It was only partially tamed by putting it into two tiny pigtails. We endured knowing looks from my dad and Colette. Well, I know I did. And Snack told me later it was the same for him. He said my dad actually chuckled in his face! Fifi and Aiden were none the wiser of our almost assignation—they were just pleased to see their father and to play with Wookiee while we had a quick breakfast.

"Hey, Gil!" Snack yells over his shoulder. My dad is once again in deep conversation with Colette.

My dad responds, "Yeah?"

"What are you doing today?"

"I don't know. Probably take Minnie to the house. Hang

around there for a bit."

Snack reaches across the table and gives my hand a squeeze, and then he stands and walks over to my dad. They sort of meet halfway and talk quietly to each other, and then Dad comes over to me.

"Mouse, Snack and I are going to go dig out the El Camino. Then I'll take you home. We need to have some time together before your date tonight." I open my eyes wide and peer around my dad. Snack heads to the door while putting on his black beanie and puffer jacket. He turns and winks at me.

"I guess he told you about that, huh?"

"Yeah, I think it's a great idea. You guys need to see more of each other. I don't know what has been going on or not going on between the two of you, but you've been apart for too long. It'll be nice to see you on a date, too, since I've never seen or met this Henry fellow of yours. I'm beginning to think he doesn't exist."

Henry. Hadn't thought of him much in the past twelve hours.

"Oh, he exists, Dad. If it's any consolation, I've never met his folks, either."

I finish my breakfast and take my plate and mug to Colette, who gives me a Snackenberg hug and a smirk. Jeez! All this smirking and winking, what the hell is going on?

"So happy you're here, sweetheart." I briefly remember what it's like to have a mom. At least what I *think* it should be like to have a mom.

I'm starting to get the feeling Dad didn't bring me home

just to catch up with an old friend. No. I think I might be on some sort of Princess-Leia-rescues-Han-Solo-from-carbonite type mission.

I awkwardly back out of the hug. "Me, too." I turn and pick up Wookiee and scramble up the stairs. I throw my clothes in my weekend bag and check around the loft to be sure I've not left anything. Wookiee supervises the entire process from his perch atop a pillow that fell off the bed.

Once I've got everything, I cursorily make the bed and head back downstairs.

Dad and Snack are coming in the front door—both laughing.

I wonder what they were laughing about.

"Oh, good. You're ready to go," Dad says to me.

"Yep, Just need to put on my coat... and—"

Wookiee barks.

"And...Wookiee's..."

Dad chuckles once more, then squats down and pats Wook on the head. "You're ready to go, too, I guess, big man."

Snack calls the kids and tells them to get ready to leave. They grumble and ask once more if the dog is coming to their house, but comply with Snack's directive.

As I walk up to Snack and Dad, my father picks up Wookiee and takes him over to Colette. I hear them talking but can't make out what they are saying.

Snack wraps his hand around my upper arm and pulls me in front of him. "I'm going to take the kids home. After you talk to your Dad, I'd like to come over. Maybe, you could, uh, trim this beard up for me before our date? I've kind of let myself go." I've always cut my dad and brother's hair, but never a beard. Talk of facial hair reminds me of Henry for a brief moment. He's so fucking particular about his mustache he goes to a barber to have it done.

"Um, sure… I'll give it a t-try," I stutter. I don't know why I stutter. Maybe it's the impending task of cutting *his* beard, Snack's blue eyes boring down into mine right at this moment, or his hand gripping my arm like he'll never let me go? The cumulative effect is my current halting speech pattern and a growing need to touch him, kiss him. And have him doing the same to me.

Snack kisses me on the forehead—a soft lingering kiss. I close my eyes and let the warmth of his lips send neurons firing all over my body, straight down to my toes *and somewhere slightly higher*. The moment is far too brief as we're quickly surrounded by parents and kids and a dog. There is a flurry of organized chaos as we leave, sans Colette who stays behind to man the café. We make our way to our respective vehicles—the kids begging for Wookiee to come to "their house" for the day. Snack and I exchange a small smile.

***

The house smells different. It looks like my childhood home, but it smells different and it looks empty and a bit neglected.

I place Wookiee on the floor and he scampers off to explore the split-level. Turning to my dad, I must have a big question mark plastered on my face.

"Min… let's… uh, let's talk. I'll turn up the thermostat and get the place warmed up. Why don't you put your stuff down and we can sit and talk."

Dad does just as he says. He dials up the heat. I hear it click on and immediately smell the lack of use of the furnace in the stale air. Nobody has been living here—at all.

Dad takes off his hat and coat and drapes them over the railing. He's being evasive. His eyes are downcast and he's avoiding mine.

Now, I'm afraid. Is something wrong with him? Is he broke? Sick? I feel an odd shaky feeling in my chest. What's with all the whispered discussions with Colette? "What's up, Daddy? What's going on?"

I've really never experienced my father so anxious. After pacing back and forth and apologizing for the condition of the house, he finally gets to the point.

"Minnie, I don't really live here anymore…"

"Is something wrong? Are you losing the house? How come you didn't tell me? I know I haven't visited in a few months, well, more than a few months, but I didn't realize… What happened? What's going on?"

Dad hems and haws and then says, "Since Sid moved out in the fall the house has been too big and…" But then he comes out with the real reason. "You know Colette has been alone since Bob cheated on her and she kicked him out eight years ago?"

"Yeah."

"Well, we've gotten closer and closer since then. Clip was gone. You were *really* gone. Snack rarely came home. The only one around was Sid, and he was so involved with his friends and video games and that noise he calls a band—"

"Dad, they're actually really good. I've heard them play in the city," I interject out of sheer nervousness.

Sid. We never called him Sidney. He was Sid. Sidney was a name more commonly associated with dashing African American actors and film producers with thick trimmed glasses or more morosely, with a murdered punk rocker— not with someone like my precious, obnoxious, redheaded baby brother. And yet it fit him perfectly.

"I know. My point *is* Colette was lonely and I was, too. We gravitated toward each other. First, it was just spending time together, but now—" And then Dad finally blurts. "I love her and she loves me." He looks at me, eyebrows raised in apprehension of my response.

"That's a *good* thing, right? Why do you look scared, Dad?"

"I just didn't know how you'd feel about it. You haven't been home much. You've been avoiding Downers Grove and Snack for years. We only got together as a family for Christmas this year for dinner. In a hotel. I just didn't know the right time to tell you. And then Snack came home after Megan died, and I was over at Colette's all the time and—"

"You want to know what I think? About you being with Colette?"

Dad sheepishly replies, "Yeah."

"I think…" I need to put this poor guy out of his misery. This is really great news. I'm happy my dad has found someone. He's been alone for so long and he's never dated before as far as I know. "I think it's great! Why didn't you tell me sooner?"

"I don't know. I wanted to be sure. I was afraid you'd never come home because of Colette being Snack's mother. I don't know. I was being stupid."

"Dad, it's OK. I understand. Sometimes it's hard to know what's going on in a relationship or how to define it or even explain it to yourself, let alone people outside of it. Really, I'm so happy for you."

My dad's face lights up with a smile of relief. "Thank you. I feel so lucky to have found Colette. I never thought I'd be in love again.

It's wonderful and also a bit weird to hear my dad talk about being in love. It also sparks a little flame of hope for me and my bizarre love history.

I suddenly have a thought. "The boys?"

"Yes. They know. I already told them."

They knew before I did. Not surprising since I haven't been as involved with them or my dad as I should have over the past few years.

"Minnie, I hope this isn't too much too soon, but… I'm putting the house on the market soon, probably in the spring. I've slowly been selling or moving things to Colette's. While you're here you may want to pack up whatever's left in your room."

"Good idea. It can't be that much."

"Oh, and one more thing…" Dad stands, pulling me up with him to face him. "Colette and I are getting married."

My mouth drops open. I close it because nothing comes

out and then it opens on its own again. I'm trying to think of the words to say.

"Is that legal?" I ask because I've been under the impression that my dad is still married to my mother.

Dad tilts his head and his eyebrows knit together. "Of course," he says in a confused voice. "Why wouldn't it be?"

"Aren't you still married to Mom?" I don't know why I'm stuck on this point. I just never thought about my dad getting remarried. In my mind, he was always married to my mother.

"Yeah, Minnie, I never told you. You kids had already been through so much. Mouse, I'm so sorry. The divorce became final a few years ago. Do you remember sometimes I would go away on business trips for weeks at a time and Mimi would take care of you?"

"Yeah."

"Well, I was working out how to make sure your mother was taken care of and how to get divorced. It took a long time. There are very specific rules about how long a person has to be declared… insane"—My dad gulps a few times—"before a, um, judge will grant a divorce."

I cut him off. It's my turn to confess. "I never told you, but I went to visit Mom at the hospital a few times, too. When I was back east at school. I just had to see her. It never crossed my mind to tell you about my visits. Just like you never told me about yours. I guess, I thought, since we never talked about her, we were just supposed to act like she didn't exist, but I never stopped wondering about her."

My dad lowers his head into his hands before looking up

at me again. "Yeah, I won't deny I've struggled with not keeping your mother's memory present, but the woman that was my wife and your mom was gone. I didn't want you to have any more pain."

"I know now why we never talked about her. Daddy, the first time I went to visit, she didn't know me at all. The second time she thought I was her, and she asked me how you were doing. She actually said, 'How is Gil? How are my children?'"

My dad presses the back of his knuckles against his closed eyes and swallows. Then clearing his voice he says softly and sincerely, "Minnie, I never wanted to divorce her, I was… we were so in love, but after she got so sick and the doctors told me she'd never get better, never get out, I thought maybe, just maybe I'd be lucky enough to fall in love again… and now I have. Is it OK with you?"

I'm shocked and pleased and happy for him. I fling myself into my his arms. "Of course it's OK. It's better than OK. It's terrific. Congratulations!" I can't help but think about my mother. I never really had her, but now I'll have a new mother. Someone that's been a de facto mother to me without me ever acknowledging it.

Then my selfish thoughts fly to the fact that I will also have a new brother. Well, stepbrother.

***

Instead of Snack coming over to have his beard trimmed, Dad suggests I go back with him to Colette's house and drop him off. Then I can have the El Camino for the rest of the day and tonight.

When we arrive, with Wookiee in tow, I'm greeted like a long lost relative, or rather, Wookiee is. Fifi and Aiden immediately get on their knees to greet him as he prances up to them, more than willing to suck up their adoration. Dad guides them all out of the living room and into the family room.

I'm about to join them when a bare foot Snack rounds the corner wearing a Stanford hoodie and jeans. He looks sleepy and tousled like he was taking a nap. I'm instantly attuned to my body reacting to how sexy and at ease he looks.

Snack runs his hand through his hair, yawns, and says, "Hey, I didn't expect you. I thought I'd go over to your house after Gil came back." Snack tilts his head, raises his eyebrows, and shrugs. "Sooo, what do you think?"

I'm confused for a moment. What do I think? About what? Then it hits me. Oh, what do I think about my dad and his mom?

"I think it is great. I had no idea."

"Neither did I 'til I showed up here with the kids. It was pretty obvious they were together when I caught them making out against the kitchen counter."

"Oh, no." I try to push the visual from my mind.

Snack nods and makes a faux horrified face. "Oh, yes!

"Why didn't you tell me last night?" I scold.

"It wasn't my news to tell."

"Yeah, I get that."

"Hey, how about that trim?" Snack runs his hand over

his unkempt beard as he approaches me.

"Sure."

"I know it doesn't look like it, but I did wash it this morning." He takes my hand and walks me to the bathroom.

"You're in luck. My dad still had the scissors I used to use to cut the guys' hair when they were younger."

When we enter the bathroom, Snack pulls his hoodie over his head and hangs it on the hook on the back of the door. He shuts the door all the way, closing us in. He has a white T-shirt on underneath. It's fitted and I can make out the contours of his biceps, shoulders, firm chest and slim waist. If I hadn't gulped a couple of times I probably would've drooled. The bathroom is a relatively small space, and I can't seem keep my eyes off his body. When I finally do look up, I feel myself flush.

"What?" Snack smirks.

"Oh." I giggle awkwardly. Snack caught me staring. "Um... so, sit down..." I point to the toilet seat. Snack does as he's told. After retrieving the scissors from my bag and placing them on the vanity, I drape a towel around Snack's shoulders. Just as I'm about to step away he grabs my wrists and places my hands on his chest. I inhale sharply upon touching him. The zing is so strong I catch myself wondering if he's a human defibrillator.

Snack wraps his hand around the back of my neck, bringing my face down to look me right in the eyes. "Have I told you how happy I am that you ca... that you're here?" Snack says in a low voice.

"Yes, you did."

Snack pulls me down closer and gives me a soft kiss on one corner of my mouth, and then the other, lingering a bit longer with the second. He retreats a hair and is about to kiss me again right on the lips. He is a fraction of a centimeter away when my fingers flex into his chest and I push away.

"No, sir." I wag my finger at him. He tries to pull me back, but I brace my hand on his shoulder. "We'll never leave this bathroom if you keep that up."

By some miracle, I manage to keep my cool and my hands off Snack long enough to trim his mustache and beard to a more manageable closer to the chin length. Less ZZ Top, more coffee house patron. Seems appropriate for someone partially raised in one. But keeping my hands to myself, doesn't mean I can't take every opportunity to brush against him with the back of my hand, straddle his thigh to get at the right angle or graze his arm with my breast. Snack let's out low growls with each "accidental" touch.

Beard trim finally complete, I announce. "There! All don—"

Snack snatches the scissors from my hand, carefully places them on the vanity, and while slipping the towel from his shoulder, he pulls me down so that I'm straddling him. His hardness is immediately against my warmed core. I run my fingers through his beard and then his hair, enjoying the thick, plush silkiness of them both. Snack sighs and his whole body sags. I sense the tension floating off him as I press myself into him—my chest against his, my thighs at his hips—and then gyrate.

Our lips crash into each other with ever more urgency.

Snack runs his tongue along the seam of my lips, entreating me to open for him, which I do without resistance. Our tongues find one another and dance so naturally. We occasionally stop to allow for a bite of a lower lip. I move my hands from his hair down to his hard, sculpted shoulders and biceps. Snack shakes his firm grip of my body to cup one of my breasts. When he rakes his thumb across my pebbled nipple, I moan. Perhaps a little too loudly.

"Snack," I say between kisses.

"Huh?" he replies, breathless.

"You live up to your name. Fucking delicious."

"I can't wait to find out how you taste, Min."

That. Right There. That's classic Snack! Completely plain words, dripping full of sex.

I'm ready to rip off my clothes right in the guest bathroom and let him find out. I wonder how his beard will feel. Down there.

"You know what this reminds me of?" Snack kisses my neck between every few words.

I nod and say SWCO at the same time he does. We both laugh into our kisses and get lost in the feeling of being together again when, like tiny clairvoyants knowing something is going on, the kids pound on the bathroom door.

"Daddy, are you in there?"

I jump in his arms, but Snack holds me to him.

There's more banging on the door. "What. Are. You. Doing? Come Out!" Fifi's little voice sounds irritated.

"Minnie, there seems to be a disturbance in the Force."

He winks. A Star Wars reference—perfect. The guy has learned. Then he directs his comments to the door. "I'll be right out, guys."

Snack rests his forehead on my shoulder. I can feel his breath like a hot breeze on my breasts. "Aaaaah! I'm going to lose my mind, if I can't be alone with you soon."

I laugh because he's never said truer words.

***

I drive myself home in the El Camino and arrive a horny mess. I'm seriously considering using the toothbrush or shower massage at this point. I decide to wait and take it all out on Snack on our date. I have a feeling from our powder room make out; he's probably feeling the same way right now. Our chemistry is real.

No so with Henry. After last night and today in the bathroom with Snack, it has become abundantly clear to me. I need to break things off with Henry.

Wookiee is staying over with Dad, Colette, and the kids tonight so I'm all alone in my childhood home. In order to occupy myself—and keep my hands out of my pants—I start packing up my bedroom. There isn't much left. Apart from my bed there is only a few drawers and shelves to clean out. Mostly books, knickknacks, and boxes of memories. While going through one of them I run across a picture of Snack and me from prom. We were so young and in love, dressed in our formal clothes. It makes me wonder what I should wear tonight. Finding my phone, I shoot Snack a text.

Minnie: I forgot to ask where are we going?
Snack: I'm not telling you.
Minnie: Well, what should I wear?
Snack: Something I'll like.
Minnie: Oh!
Snack: Bring a warm coat. I have a surprise. Only 3 more hours!

I chew my lip rereading his texts. Something he'll like? And a warm coat? What in the world are we doing tonight? What do I have that he would *like*? I abandon my packing and dig through my weekender. I hope I brought something that will work. By the time I get to the bottom of it I'm pretty sure I have it nailed! I'm so excited I start getting ready even though Snack won't be here for quite awhile.

I take a bath, partially because I love the tub at this house and partially to avoid the temptation of the shower massage. The bath allows me time to relax and think and pamper myself. After pulling my hair up high in a pony, I use some of the designer shower gel I brought with me and whip up a mountain of bubbles. I shave every possible place I think Snack might see—or touch—and then I lean back and close my eyes. A brief thought of Henry and our apartment comes to mind, but exits just as quickly. My mind and body seem to be fully centered on tonight and what it will hold.

After luxuriating for quite a while in the tub, I get out, dry myself, and then place a small dab of perfume on every pulse point I can think of: my wrists, my neck, my cleavage, behind my knees. For good measure, even though I'm not sure it's a pulse point, I put a dot right below each of my hipbones.

My outfit is all planned so I fix my hair, cajoling the stick straight stuff into my usual long bob, but with a bit more curve and texture. I keep my makeup simple but sexy.

Fortunately, by some miracle in my hurried packing, I somehow managed to throw in a matching bra and panty set. They aren't black or lacy or fancy at all. They are nude with satin banding of the same color and a small bow between the cups of the bra and another at the top of the back of the panties. I hope Snack wants to see them. I hope he *likes* them!

Chapter 13
2000 – Breakup

"I love you." The words just pop out of my mouth.

Not at any special time. Just after making out in Snack's basement. Two days before I'm about to leave for college. I didn't intend for them to slip out, but they did.

Snack's response? "I know."

Very Han Solo of him, I must say, but then he got very quiet, took three slow deep breaths, and said, "Sometimes, I think I miss her." Miss her? Miss who? Charlotte? Wait, what?

Am I really hearing this? All I can say is, "What?" Then I start fucking crying!

Snack, in a crappy attempt to clarify, tells me again, "I miss her."

I'd always been able to talk to Snack when we're alone. Never any awkwardness. But when he said he missed Charlotte right after I confessed my love for him, a wall went up with the rapidity of a Jedi waving his hand. I could see him talking to me, but the message wasn't coming through. This didn't make sense.

I stand and promptly walk to the door, straightening my clothes as I do. He basically just broke up with me. "I know? I just told you I love you and you say you know? Then you tell me you miss Charlotte in the same breath? When I said, 'What?' it wasn't because I didn't understand," I snap.

Snack scrambles to his feet and approaches me. "I don't know if I really miss her. I... I just feel guilty about her dying... And college is starting..." Snack's voice has a bit of an edge when he says his final words. "Besides, you're leaving me anyway..."

We've never talked about what would happen once we went to college. Me to Middlebury in Vermont, him to Northwestern. Is he breaking up with me because of Charlotte or college? Shit, I'm confused.

"Are you breaking up with me?" When he just looks at me, I huff, turn and spit my thoughts at him, "Now? You're doing this now?" I hammer the thought in my head at how cruel he's being. "You're breaking up with me because I'm going to college? You're going away, too!"

Snack stares at the floor in front of my feet. "You're going far away—across the country. I'm just moving fifty miles. I just can't stand the idea of you so far away."

Heaving sobs shake my body. "So, you're breaking up with me? Just like that? We aren't even going to discuss this?" This is not the moment I was expecting after saying I love you. "I gotta go before my fucking eyes get too puffy to drive."

Reaching out toward me Snack says softly, "Let me drive you home."

I pull away from him. "No, I've got to get used to not having you…" I stifle a sob. "Not having you around."

"You *are* the one leaving!" Snack shouts. I can't tell if he's angry or frustrated or what.

I give it right back to him. "And you *are* the one breaking up!"

Snack shakes his head. "We will never be broken up. Ever."

"What the fuck does that mean? Whatever! We'll be 'friends,'" I say angrily with air quotes. I take in a huge breath. I can't stay here and listen to any more of this, but I refuse to let him see me fall apart, and I'm really about to fall apart. Sarcasm drips from my voice when I tell him, "I'll send you Christmas cards." The tears are going to overwhelm me soon.

"And Snack, when you get those Christmas cards, you should know it's not just a Christmas card. When you get it you should know, someone remembers you. The you I thought you were, not the coward you are in this moment! My heart is fucking broken! I never in a million years thought you'd do this to me! I thought you loved me… I thought—"

I press my palms against my eyes, hard and then turn and leave, whispering to myself, "You were my best friend. You were supposed to be the one."

Snack calls, "Minnie!" but I don't turn around.

"Good-bye," I say over my shoulder and walk out.

***

I didn't see Snack the next day or most of the day after that. He showed up at the train station as I was waiting to leave to get to the airport.

I'm standing on the platform, talking to my dad and Sid

and telling my crazy red-headed brother how much I'm going to miss him, when I sense Snack. My Extra-Snack-Perception is confirmed by Sid looking up over my shoulder, waving a quick hands-up wave and then swiftly turning away from me.

"Minnie?" Snack's voice is rough and cracks. "I'm sorry. I didn't mean it. I don't miss Charlotte. I miss you. I miss you and you're not even gone. Do you hate me for the other night?

He's so sincere and his eyes look red and puffy like he's been crying, but it doesn't matter. We broke up and I've always held the belief that if someone breaks up with you, there is no going back. It's over. I frown and shake my head. "No, I don't hate you. I so don't hate you. But I can't be with you anymore. I can't be the girl that dated the dead girl's guy anymore. I can't stay here." My eyes start to fill with tears and I can feel my chest shaking. This is difficult. I mean, seriously, what did I expect? That we'd be together forever? I'm working really hard to repress the sobs building in my throat.

Snack looks at the ground and then up at me. "Neither can I."

I'm confused. "What?"

"I'm not staying in town after all. I'm going to Stanford. I got a letter the day we fought. They bumped me up from the waitlist. Minnie, I swear we'll call each other. E-mail. We'll see each other at Thanksgiving.

"It doesn't matter we're still broken up."

"Nope."

"What the fuck?"

"Never broken up. We're never *broken up!"*

He leans in and kisses me. I know it's the last one we will have. I don't know what it means to him, but to me it is a real good-bye kiss. My brain screams, "Let me go, Snack!" in an attempt to convince my heart, but I don't say the words aloud.

And with that, I essentially ghosted from Snack's life. From that moment forward, I would only haunt Downers Grove for a few hours at a time, rarely spending the night. Sure, my family lived there, but for a long time, it was too painful to be there. I didn't see him that first Thanksgiving. I stayed in Vermont.

Chapter 14
2014 – The Date

I open the door to let Snack in and find him with his back to the door waving at the Honda Odyssey pulling away from the curb. I can easily make out my dad, two small blond heads, and a little Yorkie face staring back. Aiden is smiling and waving, Fifi is not.

He slips through the door. "Could there be anything more awkward than being over thirty and being dropped off in minivan by the father of your date, your children, and a dog in tow to observe the whole event?"

"Oh yeah, really sets the tone for the evening." I tease.

"Let's start over…," he says. Before I have time to agree, Snack strides up the stairs, wraps his arm around my waist, and tugs me up against him. "Guess I'll just have to work extra hard to wipe that memory from your consciousness."

And with that he leans down, never breaking eye contact and licks, nips, and then sucks my bottom lip with fervor. A whimper slips out of me and it seems to fuel our kiss. Snack palms the back of my head, holding me to him. I, in contrast, seem to have lost control of my limbs. Seriously, I'm so… so… I don't even know. My arms hang limply at my sides. My brain screams at me to reach up and put my arms around his neck, but I'm focused on kissing and tasting him, and I've apparently become motorically impaired. Once my brain catches up, I place my hand on his tensed, muscular upper arm. When I touch him he breaks the kiss and steps back.

"How come I didn't spend more time kissing you?" he asks breathlessly. "I was really stupid back then."

I laugh out loud. "We actually kissed a lot, Snack." I step toward him, but Snack retreats, holding his hands up to stop me.

"Minnie, if you touch me, we'll never go on this date."

The thought of taking with him right here on the landing is not unappealing. I move toward him again. "That's OK," I say with meaning.

"No, no, no! No, it's not! We're *not* making out on the landing or in your bedroom. I have more planned for you. I have a lot to make up for. Get your coat and give me the keys to the car."

He's really taking charge tonight. "So bossy. I like it!"

I already had my coat draped across the railing, so I grab it, put it on, dig in the pocket, and hand Snack the keys to the El Camino.

When he turns away, I can't resist and I reach forward and grab his butt.

Over his shoulder, Snack says, "So grabby. I like it!" He

then leans in and adds, "I also like what you're wearing!

I have on skinny jeans tucked into tall black boots with tall lugged heels and a black deep V-neck cashmere tunic. The fact that he likes my outfit and I've pleased him, makes me smile.

Snack reaches over and takes my hand. He brings it up to his lips and kisses each one of my knuckles. Then, head still bowed, he lifts his hooded eyelids. "Ready?"

I could easily say, "More than you know," given the fluttering in my chest and the growing need in my core, but I don't. I simply whisper back in a low tone, "Oh, yes."

Snack smiles and tugs me down the stairs to the door. "Then let's go!"

***

We drive north on the highway for about twenty minutes. I repeatedly ask Snack where we're going, to which he repeatedly replies, "You'll see." In between asking, I listen to the radio and play catch-up with Snack.

"I've read some of your stuff online. I'm so glad you've gotten to do what you love. You always did such a great job with the school paper, Minnie."

"It seems I've become the Jeanne Moos of indie hipster narrative journalism." I've been very lucky to have had jobs at a string of progressive papers and magazines covering all kinds of news and features. "My favorite thing to write is a small obscure story that tugs at your heart. The tiny tales that are secretly epic." I don't tell him, but I think our story is just that.

Snack plans to stay in Downers Grove permanently. He left his job as a mechanical engineer with a big motor company in Dublin, Ohio with enough savings to spend a few months getting the kids adjusted and settled. He says he's not sure where he'll work next, but is being recruited heavily by a Chicago automotive consulting firm. Evidently, he was the head engineer for much of the inner workings of some of the most popular cars sold in America. I've been so removed from Snack, I had no idea how very successful he'd become.

When the song "Fall For You" by Secondhand Serenade comes on, the first lyric stops both our chatter. The singer sings about the night he fell for his girl all over again. The sentiment is so familiar, I feel myself blush. Snack turns the radio up. Then he takes my hand and runs his thumb across my palm. His every touch makes me wish I'd pushed the issue back at my dad's house and insisted he make love to me there. My mind is not on dinner at all.

We pull into the lot of a very busy suburban mall. I'm growing more confused by the moment. This can't be right. I'm about to give Snack a heap of verbal teasing when he stops at a valet parking sign. Not what I expected at a mall that is advertising LEGOLAND and Rainforest Café.

"Welcome to Ginza Pub," the skinny teenaged valet says as he opens my door. When I look behind him I see a small restaurant with the name. Snack walks around the car to join me. I hear the valet enthusiastically say, "This car is *so* cool," as he gets in the El Camino and drives away.

Snack ushers me into Ginza Pub by guiding me with a

hand on the small of my back. Even through my coat and tunic, it still makes me shudder a bit.

Ginza Pub is small and dark with about ten tables of varying heights. The décor and feel is a combination of high-end Tokyo nightlife and izakaya pub. Sort of classy, uptown meets casual dining. Throughout are neon signs for Japanese beers, large posters of more traditional geishas, and samurai scenes mixed with modern posters of concerts on the gray walls. The low lighting makes it intimate, while the house music fills the space with energy. I love it immediately.

"This place is unexpected in a strip mall," I whisper loudly to Snack once we've stowed our coats and are seated. I can either move closer to him and whisper in his ear or yell over the table. The first option is much more appealing and I have a sense Snack planned it that way.

"Yeah, I found it by accident when I first moved back. The kids don't like sushi and I needed to get away from being *daddy* for a few hours. Don't get me wrong. I love my kids—more than anything."

I smile at him. I'm pleased he loves his kids so much.

Snack clears his throat and puts his arm around the back of my chair. "More than anything—so far." I turn to him so our faces are inches apart. His pupils are dilated and his irises are a deep midnight I've not seen before. "Anyway," he continues, "I came here on a recommendation for some sushi and a beer. The whole time I was here I kept thinking how great it would be to share this experience with someone. I was hoping you'd appreciate it when you agreed to go out with me tonight."

"We haven't even eaten yet and I already like it."

"Just wait until you've had the food. You may not want to leave."

I reach up and stroke Snack's beard and run my thumb across his bottom lip, a lip I'd like to suck into my mouth right now. "I doubt that very much."

Snack shifts in his chair. I hope I'm affecting him the way he's affecting me.

A young Asian-American waiter, who not by accident I'm sure, looks like an anime character, interrupts our canoodling. He has a tall jet-black hairdo and huge eyes.

"Welcome to Ginza Pub!" he says. "I'm Ren. I'll be your server tonight. We work as a team here, so you'll meet lots of other servers. Just ask any of them if you need anything throughout your meal, OK? What can I get you to drink?"

Snack orders us Sake bombs. I've not had one since college, and I hope I remember how to do it without ruining my clothes. He also orders something called flying tiger shrimp tacos without even looking at the menu.

After Ren sets up our drinks with a shot of sake balanced on chopsticks above our Sapporo beers, I ask for a brief refresher. He gives us a few pointers and moments later we're banging on the table, counting in Japanese, *ichi, ni, san,* until the shot glass falls into the beer. Snack and I both yell *Bomb!* and immediately down the drinks. When I slam the glass back down on the table, the room spins. Hmm, maybe I should've eaten first. Ren asks if we'd like another and we both decline. I order a large water and another Sapporo. Snack orders a Coke. I shoot him a look.

"I'm driving and we don't want to have to call a cab, do we?" he whispers in my ear.

"Absolutely not", I think but don't say. When I look at him and nod, his eyebrows raise and a devilish look crosses his face.

After perusing the menu a bit more, we order several kinds of sushi and a hot rocks. Hot rocks is just what the menu says. Hot round river rocks on a bed of rock salt are delivered to your table and you lay pieces of meat or fish on it to cook it to the level of doneness you like.

Our dinner is fun and interactive. Cooking the food at our table and sharing plates makes for lots of opportunities to touch and feed each other with chopsticks.

Ren comes back and asks, "Would you like a happy ending?" I look at him incredulously. Snack laughs aloud. Ren laughs too and quickly calms my fears. "Don't worry, a happy ending is just what we call dessert here at Ginza Pub."

Snack tells Ren that we just need that check. "We'll save the *happy ending* for later." I punch Snack on the shoulder.

Ren lifts an eyebrow. "I see."

I punch Snack once again.

He rubs his arm and laughs again. "What? I meant dessert!"

I have to say his ability to get me riled up is masterful—in every way.

Back in the car I start quizzing Snack about our next destination and he finally tells me, "I know a better place for a happy ending." I decide not to punch him again. It hurt my hand.

***

I can tell by landmarks that we're headed back to Downers Grove. Once we turn off the highway to another area filled with shopping malls, I have a feeling deep inside that I know exactly where we're going. My gut feeling is confirmed when we pull up in front of Baskin-Robbins. Our Baskin-Robbins. From years ago.

"Perfect," I say as Snack parks the car.

"I thought you might like it," he says as he helps me out of the car. Again he has his hand on the small of my back and is holding on to my other to insure I don't slip and fall in the icy parking lot. When we pass by the curb where we first kissed, I notice the mailbox is decorated in a wrap to make it look like R2-D2. I shake my head.

Snack must notice. "What?"

I chuckle. "This could be the most perfect date ever."

We stop next to the mailbox. "I'm glad you think so. I'd love to stay out here and kiss you next to this droid mailbox all night for the sake of nostalgia, but I think we'd both freeze. So how about one kiss and then we'll go in and get that happy ending—I mean, dessert."

He barely finishes the word dessert before my lips meet his. Our lips are cold, but quickly warm to each other. My brain travels back to our first kiss, virtually sighs, and then switches direction and starts to fantasize about what could be in the very near future. What *this* kiss could lead to.

I can sense neither of us wants to stop kissing, but Snack shows some restraint and between kisses says, "Let's. Get.

That. Jamoca Almond Fudge."

It's only my laugh that ends the lip lock.

It's nine o'clock at night and Baskin-Robbins is packed. Why are all these families getting ice cream in the dead of winter? On top of the families, the entire Downers Grove Synchronized Ice Skating Team is there. I can tell by their overly made up faces and heavily styled hair that they must have just had a show and are celebrating. A few people stop and talk to Snack. I go pretty much unnoticed. I must look different than I did back in high school. Snack orders our ice cream. The exact same order we'd made when we were twelve.

Snack looks around the shop and tilts his head down to talk to me. "I don't know about you, but I don't want to sit in Baskin Robbins with all of our former classmates and their spawn. Let's get out of here."

"Are you sure?"

"Yes, I can drive and lick."

Wow, I think my Daiquiri Ice just melted in my hand. Not trying to be too anxious or obvious, I inquire, "More date?"

Snack takes a long, purposeful lick of his ice cream and swallows. "Much more date."

***

We arrive in downtown Downers Grove, and Snack drives around looking for a parking place. It seems the old sports bar down the street has been transformed into a new bar/restaurant called Whiskey, Beer and Barbeque, and it has become very popular. It must be doing a brisk business tonight because parking in downtown DG is at a premium. We eventually give up on street parking and settle for a spot in the commuter lot on the other side of the train tracks. I assume we're going to the new place.

We walk hand in hand back over the tracks and I realize I'm approaching my favorite place in the world—with my favorite person in the world. Once we reach the plaza, I stop. Snack keeps walking but when I stop, it pulls him back.

He turns and says nothing, but gives me an amazing smile and then pulls me in for a hug. I look over his shoulder and notice that SNACKS is closed. Usually, Collette would still be inside cleaning up. I suddenly become a bit concerned. I hope everything is OK.

"Snack!" I say suddenly. "How come the café is closed? Is everything OK? You haven't gotten a call or text or anything, have you?"

Snack steps back to release me and bends his head forward so our foreheads are touching. "Calm down, Minnie. Everything is fine. I asked Mom to close a little early tonight. I wanted us to have the place and the loft to ourselves."

"Oh." I sigh. Then I realize why Snack wanted his mother to close the place early and let out a more knowing, "Oooooooh."

Snack chuckles and kisses my forehead, and then my nose and each cheek until he finally finds my lips. And there it is. The kiss I've been waiting years for. A kiss in the cold with Snack in the shadow of the train station. My favorite place in the world. I cup his bearded jaw with my gloved hands. The kiss begins slow and sweet and builds to a hot frenetic tangle of lips and tongues. The moment is only made more special by the sound of the train passing through town and blaring its horn.

"Did you know this is my favorite place n the world?" I ask when we come up for air.

"No, I didn't," he answers, intrigue in his voice.

"It's where I was standing when I first saw your parent's place. It's where I always feel just a little hopeful and have that fluttery feeling inside that something good is going to happen."

Snack runs the back of his finger down my cheek. When he reaches my chin, he tips my face up and pins me with his heated gaze. "Don't fight that feeling, Minnie."

Although it's my favorite place, I no longer want to be here. I want to be alone. With him. I grasp his hand tightly and pull him across the street.

***

SNACKS Café is dark except for some dim puddles of light throughout the store. I follow them to the back of the store and climb the stairs to the loft. Snack is somewhere behind me. He said I could come up and get comfortable since he had to lock up and reset the alarm.

Moonlight and streetlight mingle and filter through the windows into the loft.

Walking toward the kitchen, I spy a box of baked goods with the SNACKS logo on it. There's a note on top of the box, but I can't make out what it says.

"Stop! Stay right there. Don't move," Snack commands from across the room. I freeze. "You look like an angel in this light."

I'm sure I flush fully. The room becomes hotter in a matter of seconds.

Snack strides toward me, pulling off his pea coat and beanie and flinging them onto the loveseat on his way over. I turn away from the counter to face him. He comes right up to me. So close but not touching. I'm completely under his spell, falling deeper into his gaze. Gently he slips my coat off my shoulders and down my arms. He gives me a quick peck on the lips as he drapes my coat across a barstool.

I let out a chuckle when Snack lifts me off the ground and sits me on the kitchen island.

He stands between my legs; his hands splayed out on the bar next to my thighs, essentially trapping me. Running my fingers over his beard and through his smooth thick blond hair, I pull him to me for a deep lingering kiss. I want to taste every inch of his mouth.

Never breaking our kiss, Snack unzips the long zipper of my boot. A moan slides from his lips. He does the same with the second one, and after yanking it from my foot, pulls me off the bar. I slowly transverse down his body, all of my body sliding down all of his. I'm met with a pleasant hardness against my abdomen and I gasp.

"Jesus, Min. If I get this hard just unzipping your boots, I'm in huge trouble!"

I can't stop myself from giggling. "I didn't know you

were a foot man."

"Foot man, ass man, breast man any part that's attached to you!"

Last time we were in the loft I was freezing. Now, I'm about to combust.

I reach down to take off my sweater, but Snack grips my hands. "No, let me,"

He slowly, torturously, peels my sweater up and over my head. Where it went after that? Who knows? Who cares.

"Thank you. I… I was so hot."

Snack kisses my neck and inhales right below my ear. "You *are* so hot."

I shiver. How is it possible to be this hot and shiver at the same time. Only Snack could do this to me. I've never reacted to a man in this way—ever!

He continues to kiss and suck all the way down to my shoulder. He slips the straps of my camisole down and nips at my skin. Just the same as with my sweater, my camisole soon disappears. I'm standing in the middle of the loft half naked in my bare feet, bra, panties, and jeans with a man I've longed for forever.

Snack cups my breasts with both hands. His thumbs rake across my tight and tortured nipples. When he begins unbuttoning my jeans, my reserve fails and I start backing him up.

Toward the bed.

I need his clothes off and soon. My fingers can't work fast enough to remove his navy blue button up. Snack steps back only long enough to slide his T-shirt off. My hands are immediately back on him, surveying every bulge and ripple of his muscled chest and firm abs. I'd like to get on my knees and lick them, but that would mean stopping what I'm doing. I make a note to myself do that later. After taking a tour of Snack's naked torso, I reach down to unzip his jeans, but not before palming his erection. I felt it against my stomach, now I want to feel it in my hands. I can make out the stiff shaft and turgid head even with the barrier of his Levi's.

Snack tips his head back and groans at my touch.

We tear at each other's jeans. Snack walks us backward toward the bed. I trip as my jeans gather around my ankles, flopping around like a denim octopus. I drop onto his chest and he falls back on the bed. Perfect positioning. We both scream with laughter. Not exactly the coolest seduction on either of our parts.

Between chuckles and snorts, I confess, "I… I'm just so nervous. You're so… God, you're so beautiful, and I'm so…" I squeeze my eyes shut unsure how to face my self-doubt. "What if it's not good?"

Snack shakes his head and smirks. "What are you talking about? You're beautiful. The most beautiful thing in my world. Min, it's going to be amazing!"

I run my hands over his chest again, stare at his lips, and then his eyes. "Stop reading my mind."

"Make me."

Both our jeans are off in moments, as are his boxer briefs and my panties. No more SWCO for us!

Snack wraps his large arm around my waist and, in a well-calculated twisting move, positions me horizontally on the bed underneath him. His mouth crashes down on mine and our tongues dance and swirl.

I writhe beneath him, thrusting, and gyrating against his thigh. Snack's cock is insistent against me. I want him inside me so badly.

My want is only heightened when Snack's lips leave mine and he dips his face toward my breasts. He looks back up at me quickly and arches an eyebrow, telegraphing his intent to tease me further. Again cupping and kneading my breasts, he breathes over them and I arch and groan. As I arch, Snack laves one of my nipples into his hot mouth and sucks deeply. So deeply I have to close my eyes and hyperextend my neck to handle the sensation. The excruciatingly painful pleasure shoots down to my clit, and I swear I feel it throb. Snack repeats this exquisite move again with my other breast. I claw at his back, non-verbally pleading with him to give me more. My hands slide down to his round, firm ass and I pull him toward my pelvis. I'm going to come and leave him far behind if this doesn't happen soon.

"Oh, God, Minnie. I can't wait any longer."

"Good! Be... Because I can't, either. Please, Snack. Marcus, Please!"

Snack pants. "Oh my God, you called me Marcus."

"I'm serious, Snack." I groan. "Now, please!"

Snack doesn't need more encouragement. He positions his ample cock at my entrance and just as he's about to thrust, I scream, "Wait! What about protection?"

Snack freezes in his nearly there position and looks at me

with bugged eyes. "Oh shit! I haven't needed one in so long."

Why? Because he hasn't had sex or because he was married?

"You don't have one?

Shaking his head in frustration."Nooooo!"

I lift his head with both hands and smile. "Not to worry, I do!"

"Thank the Lord, because we were going to have to resort to some Ziploc bag MacGyver prophylactic situation if you didn't! There's no way I can stop now!"

The thought of Snack's homemade birth control device is hilarious! I roll out from underneath him and reach over the side of the bed for my jeans. Years of watching my brothers' sexcapades has taught me to have one of these bad boys at the ready. You never know, but in the case of tonight's date, I sort of suspected.

I sit up and Snack kneels back on his heels. I'm presented with his gorgeous, hard, twitching cock, which I quickly sheath with the condom. This is taking far too long. As I cloak his beast, Snack slides a finger between my slickness and then his thumb joins, circling and applying pressure to my already engorged clit.

I lean back, letting him continue the delicious foreplay for a bit longer, but then I pour my need out by locking my eyes on his. Snack responds by covering me with his whole body and thrusting his throbbing erection with one long movement. We both moan at his arrival. I've waited forever for this and it's finally happened. Snack and I are finally having sex. No, not just sex. We are making love. Knowingly

Snack doesn't move. He just stays very still.

Then looking down for a long moment he softly and deeply says, "Hi!"

I giggle which causes a pleasant contraction below and then say, "Hi!" back. I've never laughed so much during sex before. It's a pretty great feeling.

And then the laughing ends. I rock into Snack with slow, rhythmic thrusts, contracting my inner most sensitive muscles with each one.

"Jeez, Minnie, you are on fire."

"Mmhmm." My powers of speech are failing. I can feel my orgasm building. It will not take long. I'm chanting something that sounds like "Please, please, please, please" as Snacks kisses up my neck to just under my ear.

"Don't worry, baby, I'll get you there." Snack meets me gyration for gyration and just as I peak and grab at the sheets, he stills and we both cry out in a deep guttural unintelligible release of emotion.

After a few long exhalations, Snack pulls out of me and I wince at the loss, immediately missing his closeness. Snack reaches around in bed and then I feel him wiping me between my legs. I can only guess he grabbed a piece of clothing from somewhere. I yawn and smile at him. His face is calm and happy in the warm glow from the ambient light.

"Why didn't we do that sooner?" I yawn into his chest.

"So many reasons," Snack whispers into my hair. "Reasons that, for the life of me, I can't recall clearly. I'm kicking myself for making us wait so long."

"We won't wait long again," I say hopefully.

Snack laughs. "No, we won't!"

Snack kisses me on the forehead and pulls me under his arm so my head is resting between his chest and shoulder. Snack gently covers me with the duvet.

Sleep comes easily.

Chapter 15
2005 – Five Year High School Reunion

People deliver platitudes like, "Always say I love you" to your spouse and children when you leave. How about the person who ignores you? Like my mother. How about the person you work really hard to like? Like Charlotte. How about the person you love, but really can't bear to be around? Like Snack? Yeah, how about Snack? I told him I loved him and look how well that worked out.

We saw each other briefly throughout college the few times I actually allowed myself to go home to Downers Grove during Thanksgiving and Christmas breaks. We talked about our separate lives but never a life together, not anymore. I don't know why we didn't go there. We just didn't.

I kept our conversations civil and shallow because talking about anything too deep would surely send me into a love-fog, and I was determined to stay clear and focused when it came to Snack. I just couldn't get past the way he broke up with me. Broke me. Although I deep down I still loved him, would always love him, he couldn't be mine. We had our time, but we were kids and the circumstances of our relationship were wrong. All wrong. There was a strained push-pull whenever we were in each other's presence.

Clip told me Snack had plenty of girls in college. I dated a few guys. Although, he never asked and I never told, Snack knew that I was no longer a virgin.

I completed four years at Middlebury, graduating with a degree in English that focused primarily on narrative journalism. Then I spent a year traveling and writing in Europe thanks to a gift from my Mimi. It was then—away from the states and well away from my family and Snack—that I finally gave myself to someone.

I was in England. His name was Teddy. He treated me very well. He was very concerned when we did it—that I really *wanted* to have sex and that he didn't hurt me. He actually asked me to stay in England with him, but when I received an invitation to my five-year high school reunion, a strange longing overtook me. I accepted the invitation and went home for the reunion. I really don't know what inspired me. Maybe it was because I was homesick and missed my family or perhaps I felt, maybe, just maybe, I could finally survive being in a room with Snack for more than an hour and for more than a cursory conversation. Whatever it was, the pull was undeniable, so I left the lovely UK Teddy and came home.

I showed up late to the reunion. I figured I'd go and if it was horrible I'd leave. When I arrived into town, I hopped a cab to the house. My father was very surprised to see me, to say the least. Sid was the only kid living at home and a junior in high school, so not home much. Dad was over the moon to see me. It had been months and overseas calling plans were expensive. I'll admit I didn't get to a Internet café to email him very often.

I probably should stay home with Dad but I don't. I quickly change into a tailored blue cocktail dress with a trumpet skirt, gather my long, brown hair up into a high pony, borrow the El Camino, and go to the reunion.

The five-year reunion for North Downers Grove High School Class of 2000 is at The Architect, a banquet venue up on Butterfield Road. The reception hall is owned by the family of a classmate of mine and is way *too nice for a bunch of pseudo adults one year out of college.*

When I arrive, I'm greeted at the reception table by none other than Lorna D'Innocenzio. Really? My nemesis is my first contact back after avoiding the place for years.

I'm shockingly pleased at how bad she looks, and almost immediately feel disgusted with myself for thinking such a meanspirited thing. How could five years change someone so much? She looks puffy and her hair is thinning. She looks much older than twenty-three.

Weirder still is that she's kind to me. No "Fugly Mouse." No intimidation.

"Minnie? Minnie Cooper? You look terrific!"

"Thanks, Lorna." I can't believe I'm thanking Lorna.

"We haven't seen you around here since graduation. The rumor mill in DG has been working overtime wondering where you've been. I bet Snack will be happy to see you. He's in rare

form tonight."

"I've been overseas. I'll be happy to see everyone, too." What am I saying? I'm not here to see anyone but Snack.

Crossing my arms loosely, I pinch myself on the soft part of my underarm because I had to be dreaming. Is Lorna actually being nice to me? And what does she mean Snack is in "rare form?"

The question no sooner floats to the top of my mind when I hear him. Over all the crowd noise and music from the DJ, I hear his voice above everything else. Deep and smooth, his voice held a distinctive rasp when he spoke low in his register to make a point.

He must have spotted me through the crowd in the lobby to the reception hall. "MY GIR—!"he shouts, but holds his tongue before he finishes. "Everyone, Minnie Cooper is here! She's decided to grace Downers Grove with her presence!"

His last statement is sarcastic, but I don't care. It's true. I haven't been around much.

In one of the most movie-like moments of my life, the crowd actually parts and Snack walks through the canyon of North Downers Grove High School alumni right up to me. There are hundreds of pairs of eyes on us.

Snack swoops me up into his arms and spins me around. "You're here! You're really here! How come you didn't tell me? Did anyone know?"

"I sent in my RSVP, but maybe it didn't arrive. The invitation just got to me a day or two before I left England. I wonder why we didn't do it electronically?"

Snack shouts out to the entire ballroom, "Who knew? Who

here knew?"

A voice from the crowd says, "I did, but not until this afternoon. I didn't want to tell you in case she was a no-show." Snack still has me in a spinning hug, and I think I our senior class president is the person that answered him.

Once Snack sets me back on my feet, I tell him, "Hey, even my Dad didn't know. I surprised him."

"Awesome surprise. Let's get a drink!" Snack grabs my hand and pulls me further into the party.

Snack had already been drinking from the subtle slur of his words.

"Minnie?" There's a very familiar voice behind me.

I turn to see another face I haven't seen in a year. Clip is here!

He lifts his chin at Snack. "Hey, man!"

Then with much more gusto he yells, "Hey, Mouse!" I'm wrapped up in yet another hug. "Dad called me. He said you snuck into town and you'd be here. I know it's not my class reunion, but I was able to talk my way past D'Innocenzio."

Of course he was able to. He's Clip Cooper. Irresistible to anyone with two X chromosomes. "Yeah, Clip, what's up with her? Why is she so nice now?

"Oh man, Minnie. She has lupus. It really changed her. She had to drop out of her courses at beauty school. Works in the library. Could you ever imagine?"

I shake my head. "No, I couldn't. I wouldn't wish that on my worst enemy—which I guess she was."

Snack pulls my arm. "Minnie! Clip! Let's go! Let's party! You can play catch up later."

I shake my head and turning so Snack can't see, I mouth, "What's up with him?"

Clip whispers in my ear. "He broke up with his girlfriend, Megan."

"Oh, Megan? Like cheerleader-from-high-school Megan?" I didn't have a negative thought in the world about Megan. She saved my ass with Lorna. Sure, she was gorgeous and popular and could have been easy to be envious of just because of those reasons, but she was never anything but nice to me. I'm not surprised Snack started dating her. I wonder how long they've been together?

"Yep."

Snack goes to the bar. He yells back at us. "Hey, what do you want? Clip? Minnie?"

"I'll have a beer." I've gotten used to drinking beer since living in Europe for the past year.

"Me, too." Clip adds.

Let's face it. Five-year reunions are lame. You're barely out of college. Half the people here went to college together at University of Illinois like Clip did, and probably saw each other yesterday. If they even completed college in four years! Most of them are in their first jobs. I shouldn't judge. I don't even have a job yet. I'm surprised by the number of married couples. Yeah, five-year reunions are lame, but I'm having a great time—dancing, laughing, and hanging out with two of my favorite guys. Occasionally someone else from my class comes up and says hi and comments on how they barely recognize me. How different I look from high school. Funny, I know I'm different on the inside than I was when I left, but don't think I look that different.

"I know," Snack tells a classmate. "She was cute in school, but man, she's smoking now! I mean look at that ass. That dress is amazing!" He high-fives the dude and then snakes an arm around my waist. Clearly, Snack is smashed. I should be offended by the ass comment, but I'm really enjoying his touch.

While I dance to Fall Out Boy with my brother, he leans in to whisper-yell over the music the details of Snack's recent breakup, but not loud enough for anyone else to hear.

"Snack has been with Megan for a pretty long time. And then Poof!—they broke up. It's strange because Snack, who was the one who did the breaking up, has been acting really down about it. Drinking a lot. Dating a lot. Well, not really dating. More Like hooking up a lot."

Hmm… maybe I've arrived back in the States at the right time.

"Kay, Clip! Izmyturn." Snack sloppily cuts in.

I immediately decide to stop drinking. I'll probably have to drive him home.

The song changes to Mariah Carey's "We Belong Together," and Snack pulls me right up against him. He may be drunk, but he holds me and dances with confidence. The words of the song cause me to inhale sharply. Mariah is singing everything I'm feeling about Snack and me belonging together.

Snack slurs when he asks, "Minnie, am I dreamin'? 'Cause I can't believe you're here. An' you loogsogood." He rubs my lower back and then pulls me even closer. He whispers in my ear, "And smell e'en better."

Any will power I thought I had when it came to Snack dissolves there and then. I'm home. He's single. I'm single. We're both out of college. This is what we were waiting for.

We pull away only enough to look each other in the eyes. Our lips are millimeters apart and as if our thoughts meld, we both say in a longing tone, "Let's get out of here."

Snack pulls me toward the door and I turn to wave goodbye to Clip. He's surrounded by all the single ladies of the North Downers Grove Class of 2000 but looks up in time to see me wave.

We only just make it to the El Camino. I turn away to open the driver's side door, when Snack removes my hands from the car door. He places my arms with his on top on the roof of the car, pushes his front against my back and gently, but intently kisses my exposed neck from my ear down to my collarbone. I'm smashed against the door handle and it's not that unpleasant, perhaps because I can also feel how aroused Snack is as his cock is hard against my ass. As quickly as he pinned me, he spins me to face him and now his hardness is even better felt!

I crash my lips onto his and we kiss, both of us holding each other's faces. It's a sensation I know well and have missed, too so much. Everything seems possible now!

When we finally part, both hyperventilating with lust and anticipation, Snack rubs his thumb across my bottom lip. "I love the way your lips look when I've kissed them—swollen and ruby red. Always have. I almost forgot that." He needn't say another word. I'm his.

And then it all comes crashing down.

"SNACK?" a high-pitched, anguished voice calls from a few cars away.

Snack and I turn toward the voice.

A petite woman with long blonde hair stands, shivering and holding her stomach.

Snack turns fully toward the blonde. "Megan? What? What are you doing here?"

She answers in a thin, ragged voice, "I need to talk to you."

Snack turns back to me and mouths, "I'm sorry." Then without looking at her says, "Really, Megan? You need to talk to me? Right now?"

"Yes!" This girl looks really pained.

Snack whisper softly, "That's my girlfriend. Well, my ex-girlfriend."

"I know. I remember Megan from school." As much as I want him to send her away, obviously something is wrong. I take a deep breath. "Go, Snack. You should go talk to her."

Snack leaves and goes to Megan, who has begun crying. He takes her in his arms and when she holds her stomach again, his eyes get big and scared. I can't hear what they're saying, but I'm coming to realize our time together is probably over. From what little I know of Megan, she's a good person and their breakup is so recent. My gut is telling me to walk away.

Snack walks Megan to a nearby car and then comes back to the El Camino. He's now quite lucid and doesn't seem the least bit intoxicated.

"Min, jeez. I'm so, so sorry, but Megan and I need to... We need to talk. Can we maybe see each other tomorrow?"

I sigh. "Yeah."

"Yeah?" Snack's voice rises with hope.

"I mean..." I shake my head. "No... So, I can't do this with you again."

"Minnie, please."

Squaring my shoulders and swallowing the tears I refuse to let him see, I make full eye contact and say, "Good-bye, Snack."

Escaping into the El Camino, I turn the key in the ignition and blaze out of the parking lot as fast as my high-heeled foot can press the accelerator. Snack's hands fly off the car where he was trying to hold on.

I don't drive far. Just over to the mall across the highway. Ironically, I park right in front of Baskin-Robbins. Our Baskin-Robbins. I pull out my phone and text Clip and then my dad.

I don't stay at my dad's that night. After dropping off the car and grabbing my clothes, I go back into Chicago with Clip. There's no way I'm staying in Downers Grove knowing that Snack is going to reject me again.

***

Clip drives. He and I are quiet until we were almost at his apartment.

He finally breaks the silence. "What the fuck happened? Last I saw you were leaving with Snack and in a pretty big hurry."

In an attempt to deflect, I apologize for tearing him away from his bevy of girls.

"Shit, Minnie. I don't care about the chicks. Just stop being so elusive!" Clip practically yells.

"Elusive. Nice word. Your vocabulary is improving."

"Fuck you, Minnie. How's that for vocabulary?" Clip takes one hand off the wheel to flip me off, causing the car to swerve.

"Shit!" Now, I've pissed him off and almost caused an accident, which means my only option is to start telling the truth.

Quiet tears slide down both my cheeks and I gulp. "I-I don't think we're meant to be together." The tears come even faster with my open verbalization of what I've been holding back for a long time—the hope that one day Snack and I would find our way back to each other—now crushed. I'm forced to tell Clip about the episode in the parking lot with Snack and how he went to Megan.

As we stop near his apartment, Clip puts the car in park. "There has to be some explanation. Snack isn't a cruel guy. He's just... He's just always trying to please everyone. Be the hero." Clip reaches over and grabs my hand.

I nod and give into the truth. "Time just isn't our ally." I break down and blubber.

Clip pulls me into a comforting brotherly hug. "God dammit, Minnie, I love you. And I love Snack. But, I don't know. It seems like you two aren't destined to be together. At first, I felt like an asshole because I kept you guys apart, but even after you got together in high school, forces just haven't been on your side. Your age. Charlotte's death. College. Fucking stubbornness on your side. And his side, too."

I laugh through my tears and hit Clip on the bicep.

"I thought, seeing you together at the reunion that maybe, just maybe this would be it. This would be your time. But now with Megan showing up... I don't know, Min."

I don't know either.

Chapter 16
2014 – Morning after THE DATE

I wake in the exact position I fell asleep in, tucked up against Snack. I look at him with only my eyes so I don't disturb him. He's beautiful. He always has been. Even when I was colossally pissed off with him or disappointed in him, that one thing remained. To me he was always the most magnificent thing I'd laid eyes on. I've struggled to push that reality out of my consciousness, but now that we've been together, *really* together, there's no denying it any longer. I am forever in love with Marcus Christopher Snackenberg. I peel my eyes from his pouty lips to take in his jawline and then drop my eyes to his firm chest. I can stare at him all day.

It was still dark with a bit of moonlight and streetlight mix coming in through the large window in the dining room and spilling onto the floor in front of the bed. It is just enough light to see the whole loft in a fuzzy filter. I wonder why I was awake and soon realize my mouth is dry. I lick my lips a few times, but the dryness doesn't improve. I need a drink of water.

I push away from Snack as delicately as I can, feeling less warm being away from the heat of his body. Even though I'm completely naked, I don't bother to put on a T-shirt and I can't steal the sheet, since it's tangled around Snack's legs. I can just grab some water and slip right back into bed next to my… What is he to me now?

I pad into the kitchen and open the refrigerator door as quietly as I can. When I turn back and step out from behind the island, I see Snack is awake. He's propped up in the bed and watching me. And biting his lip.

Standing buck naked in the middle of an open space sends a flourish of insecurity over me. I hold up the water bottle I got from the fridge. "Do you want some water?"

"No." Snack's voice is husky from sleep and what I hope is want. "I want to look at you. Don't move."

I stand. Snack's eyes on me cause my skin to instantly flush. I turn my head, as if the action of me not looking at him will make the energy buzzing between us lessen. It doesn't. My nipples harden and I swear I feel flames burning from my inner thighs up to my core.

"Do you have any idea how amazing you look right now?" Snack growls.

I continue to look to the side. I've been naked with men before, but it's never been in conjunction with the emotions I'm struggling to control right now. I can only shake my head because the lump in my throat won't allow me to vocalize.

"I've been imagining what just happened for almost twenty years."

I laugh and ask before I can stop myself, "Really, you were thinking about *that* as a twelve-year-old?" What am I thinking? Every twelve-year-old boy thinks about sex.

Snack the mind reader answers before I ask, "I don't mean just sex, I mean I imagined it specifically with you. More like when I was thirteen years old, certainly after I first kissed you. And then all summer at Lake Geneva." Still propped up in bed, Snack reaches out to me, his palm up. "Minnie, I want you to come back to my bed."

I walk slowly back to him and take his hand. My mouth drier than before, but I don't think water is what I want anymore. There's something different I have in mind to slake my current thirst.

Snack pulls me down to him but at the last minute pulls himself up and meets me halfway. His hands are in my hair, his lips are on my eyelids, my temples, my cheeks, and finally my mouth. He kisses me with long, slow strokes of his tongue that take my breath away. When we come up for air, he slides his hands from my hair to cup my jaw, thumbs on my chin. "So, I need to know... While we've been... together. Were you, maybe, thinking... about someone else?"

"What?" I squeak. "No!"

Snack gives me a lopsided smirk. "A tall dark stranger maybe? Huh? Let me give you a hint." One of Snack's hands goes to my back as he slides his other one from my jaw to my chest and splays his fingers wide above my breasts. My body completely sandwiched between his hands and under his control. He leans me back on the bed and begins humming "Darth Vader's Theme."

I lift my head and giggle. "Oh my God, you know? When did you know?"

"Oh, course, I knew. I knew right after I handed you that toothbrush. I could hear it buzzing and John Williams playing on the regular in your bedroom after that day."

"You didn't?"

"I did. It was hot."

I cock my head and smile right back at him, even though I'm sure I'm blushing furiously. "Thank you."

"Enough. Be quiet. Relax. Let me show you how much better I am than a vibrating toothbrush."

Snack pushes me back more firmly. My head hangs off the bed and I can see the reflection of us together in the mirror across the room. Snack leaves a trail of slow deep kisses from my collarbone and down between my breasts. He kneads both of them and then pinches my already sensitive nipples.

His mouth consumes my body, tasting and sucking my skin until he reaches the apex of my thighs, throbbing with need. Snack's beard tickles and scrapes against my inner thighs and along my mound until he dips his head further and licks my clit before sucking powerfully and starting into the lingual alphabet. I squeeze my eyes shut to manage the overwhelming clenching at my core. I arch to take it all in. Snack physically restrains me, grasping my hips to stop my wiggling. Oh! He. Does. Not. Stop. Humming. Not until I come violently and thrust my hands into his hair to keep him close.

When I allow him to leave, he looks up at me. His hair and beard look like an Ewok awakened from a deep sleep.

I shake my head. "Wow, that was… better than a toothbrush."

"You better believe it, young Padawan."

I can't stop the smile that spreads across my face. "And you've been brushing up on your Star Wars lingo. Very Sexy."

"I've made a point over the past few years to watch all the movies."

"Why?"

"I knew how important it was to you. Watching them made me feel close to you even when we weren't."

Snack crawls up my body and, in a lightning quick move, sits me up over his legs, straddling him. We both turn our heads to the right and stare back at each other from our reflections in the mirror.

"See how well we fit together." Snack comments.

I hum. "Uh-huh." I lower my head to the crook of his neck to inhale his deliciousness. There's a spiciness about him not unlike the cinnamon smell of the cafe.

Rocking my already soaked core against his persistent hardness is not enough. I want him. Now.

"God, Min." Snack growls into my hair, his hands flat on my back, pressing us together. His mouth is everywhere it seems. "I think I may always need a mirror when I make love to you. I swear I'm getting off just watching you move against me!"

"I bet it would be even better if you were in me."

That mere invitation sets off a firestorm. Snack's powerful arm wraps around my waist and lifts me quickly, and then just as swiftly he's in me. I cry out at the sudden fullness, but continue to tilt and release my pelvis, trying my best to take in as much of his ample cock as I can.

"Minnie, put your hands on your head."

Snack's command is so direct, I respond without delay. He then lays back, but continues to run his hand over my body from my breasts, over my stomach, and then down to where we're joined. There he stops and with both thumbs he runs slow circles over my clit, one thumb following the next in a never-ending swirl. My core clenches his hardness and then convulses, which triggers Snack to thrust up and in with even more passion. Hitting my peak, Snack is right behind me. I throw my head back and scream his name as he takes an even firmer purchase on my hipbones and powers his release deep into me.

Panting, he tells me, "I've never fit with anyone more perfectly. And I'm pretty sure you haven't either."

"You're right. I haven't."

Snack pulls out of me by lifting me off and then sits up. We're in the middle of the bed, me straddling him. Face-to-face. Completely naked and open.

"Minnie, can I tell you something?"

I laugh. We just made spectacular love and he's asking if he can tell me something? "Of course! You can tell me anything."

Snack appears pensive. "I have been so connected to you

for twenty-six years. I know I actively pushed you away when you left for college and even after that, but I could never let go."

My mouth falls open. "What do you mean 'pushed me away?' You said you missed Charlotte. You said…"

Snack drops his head so his forehead is on my shoulder, his lips brushing my collarbone. "I lied," Snack confesses. "You know why we never made love in high school? You know why I picked a fight with you right before you left for Middlebury?"

Confusion is the only word for this moment. Snack just told me he said he missed Charlotte to push me away. He said he picked that fight with me on purpose. I shake my head. "No, I don't know why. No, I can't believe that's what kept us apart."

"At first, it was Clip. All the stuff he said to me before we started dating. All his warnings lingered with me, but really it was just… straight up fear. Fear of losing you.

In the end, my fear of *really* losing you had you lost to me the minute you got accepted into college."

"Oh my God." I bring both hands to my head and shake it back and forth. What am I hearing? "I think I'm beginning to see. To you, if we never broke up, then you could never lose me. If you never made a commitment to me or even risked failing to keep the commitment, you couldn't lose me."

"Exactly."

It was twisted, illogical thinking, but it was all too human. I suppose I did the same thing, in a way. I'd never committed to anyone, or anything for very long. All that wasted time away from each other, but then again, Snack still cares about me. He never stopped caring about me. Just like I could never shake him. I'm not confused about how I feel anymore. I straighten up and poke my finger at his glorious chest. "First of all: Never listen to my stupid brother again."

Snack nods and puts his hand up like he's taking an oath of office. "I won't."

"And second: I think I understand. I was afraid of losing you, too. I had already lost you to Charlotte once. And then got you back. But when we broke up—"

"We *never* broke up. I never said those words. Why do you think I wrote NBU on every single Christmas card I sent you?"

I always wondered what that was. Why there were the letters NBU on every Christmas card, on anything, I ever received from him. NBU meant Never. Broken. Up.

"Like I was saying… *when* we broke up… I was heartbroken because I lost my boyfriend and my best friend. But I survived. Really, what was I expecting? That we'd get married at eighteen? That we wait for each other for four years during college? That we'd both give up our dream educations just to go to the same school to be together? No, my rational side understood. I survived losing my boyfriend, even though I frequently longed for you. That dream really fell apart when I thought I had another chance, but instead I wound up watching you marry Megan."

"You were there? At the wedding?"

I nod.

"I didn't know. I'm so sorry."

I change the subject. Delving into the emotions I felt during his wedding to Megan is not a place I want to revisit right now. "I've missed you, Snack. I've missed my best friend."

Snack thrusts his hands into my hair and puts his forehead on mine. His eyes close as if he's praying. "He's right here. Your best friend. Your boyfriend. Whatever you want to call me, Minnie. I'll be whatever you want."

"I just want you to be with me," I say before claiming him once again with my lips, my arms, my body.

Chapter 17
2005 – The Groom

Snack called me the day after the reunion. Milliseconds from pressing the talk button, I let it go to voice mail. I'm very glad I did because his message crushed me. I was saved from him hearing the anguish that surely would've been in my voice had I spoken to him.

"Megan and I are back together. She, um… There's no other way to say this, Minnie. Megan is pregnant. I didn't know when we broke up. She came and found me last night because she was afraid she was losing the baby…" I erased it without listening to the rest of the message.

Snack and Megan's wedding was a month after our class reunion. To say it was a rushed affair was an understatement. Many of the older invitees were probably blissfully unaware of the reason for the hurried nuptials. Megan was nine weeks pregnant.

I received my invitation and, after fighting my initial response to tear it up or burn it unopened, stuck it up on the fridge in the tiny studio apartment on Belmont I lived in at time. I looked at it every day. Snack was completely lost to me. All hope lost forever. I had to decide if I wanted to witness it or go to one or two of my favorite North Halsted dive bars to daydrink instead of hauling my miserable ass to Bolingbrook for the "blessed event."

I never RSVP.

At the last minute I decide to go. The irony isn't lost on me that the wedding is being held at St. Benedict's, because I feel like a complete traitor to my heart.

I wait across the street, watch the last of the guests file in, and sneak in through a door on the side of the church. I can hear the organ music playing as I wind my way through a few empty Sunday school classes and up the stairs that lead to the back of the church.

Fortunately, there are side aisle doors in the back of the church for me to sneak in. All eyes are on the bride as she makes her way down the center aisle. Nobody notices the chick dressed all in black at the back of the church hiding behind a pillar. Nobody except Adam Peterson. My ill-fated homecoming date.

"Hey, Cooper," Adam whispers as he approaches. "Black to a wedding, huh? Classy."

"Yeah, I really should stop taking my fashion inspiration from Darth Vader."

"I think you look great."

I shush him and then tilt my head quickly toward the front of the church to indicate for him to shut up and listen. I don't want to hear whatever else he had to say.

From my hiding place I can make out the back of my dad's

head and Colette's. Sid's red mop of hair was a flaming beacon. And then there was my far-too-good-looking-for-his-own-good big brother, Clip. Standing up next to Snack. The best man. I snicker silently as I think to myself, "The best man to nail every bridesmaid in sight, is more like it."

I swear I don't breathe more than three times over the next twenty minutes as I watch the only man I've ever loved marry somebody else. Really, it is the matrimonial equivalent of rubbernecking at a fatal accident on the highway. It leaves me nauseated and light-headed. I already regret my decision to not take up residence on a barstool all day.

Snack kisses his bride.

The pastor announces, "Ladies and Gentlemen, may I introduce Mr. and Mrs. Marcus Snackenberg." The congregation breaks into applause.

With that, I turn to Adam. "Let's get the F-U-C-K out of here." I figure I'd better spell out the F-word since I'm in a church and all.

I didn't stick around to talk to my dad or Sid or Clip or anyone besides Adam that day. I'm pretty sure no one else saw me there. As far as Snack's wedding was concerned—I was never there.

Adam and I jump in his Toyota Corolla and hit Day N' Night on the way back to Downers Grove. We buy a fifth of Jack Daniel's simply because I want to get drunk and Adam is sick of going to weddings, so that's as good a reason as any to join my pity party.

While Snack and his new bride and the rest of my family were partying at the local country club, I was hunkered down at three o'clock on a beautiful fall Saturday afternoon in Adam's crappy little apartment above the cigar shop in downtown DG. Adam went to University of Illinois and graduated, but never really left Downers Grove. As a matter of fact, he's now a writer, reporter, and photographer for the local paper, *Suburban Life*, which documents all the doings of the western Chicago suburbs. When he told me, he also informed me that we were going to have to make up some shit about the Snackenberg reception, because he was supposed to be detailing the whole wedding and after party for the newspaper. It was nice of him to add that he'd much rather be drinking with me. I agreed to help him fabricate the details.

With all honesty I can report that I had no idea how many shots of Jack I did that afternoon. I had every intention of having a few Jack and Cokes and then hopping the train back to the city. That all went out the window when Adam failed to mention he had no Coca-Cola at his apartment, and I decided it would only slow down the much-needed numbing process.

I kick off my shoes and curl my legs up under me in one corner of Adam's futon. Bottle of Jack in one hand, a Welch's grape jelly jar glass in the other. Adam chooses a plastic measuring cup as his drinking vessel. It's not surprising to me that the entirety of Adam's drinkware is comprised of jars, plastic tumblers from bars, or some form of cooking equipment. If he'd offered me dinner, I'm pretty sure I'd be eating ramen from a re-purposed Cool Whip container. I wonder for a moment why I'm here instead of at a plated wedding reception.

But only for a moment. I know I'd never be able to sustain a civil demeanor, let alone stay sober and keep from vomiting if I'd had to watch Snack's first dance with his new bride.

To avoid discussing the wedding, Adam and I drink from midday until sunset or until the fifth is obliterated. Or should I more accurately say, we *are obliterated.*

"Well," I slur as I make an attempt to extricate my legs from under my body, "I gezz I shood go!"

The minute my feet hit the floor, my knees and then my face quickly join them as I plant it on the hardwood.

"Shit! My fucking legs are asleep!" I force myself to gain control of my al dente noodle extremities and push myself up onto all fours. I very ungracefully shove myself back until I plop on my ass, grateful that the couch is propping me up. I begin laughing like a madwoman.

Adam is completely entertained by my futon dismount and chuckles. He crawls his intoxicated way across the apartment to slide down next to me on the floor.

"Minnie, you are the funnest and funniest chick I've ever known."

"Funn-est is not a word."

"Fuck that. I'm a writer; you *are a writer. We have creative license. Funn-est is so a word."*

I rest my head on Adam's shoulder and close my eyes. He reaches over and strokes my cheek. Then he runs his thumb down my jaw and turns me to face him. I feel his lips touch mine and immediately open my lips and allow Adam to consume me. It's nice. Nice to be kissed. Nice to be numb.

In the midst of our lip smashing, Adam chuckles. "I don't

think Snack's going to break in and stop us this time," he says, recalling our thwarted homecoming make-out session in the journalism room. The one that ended with me becoming Snack's girl and, eventually, Adam and Charlotte's accident.

I agree. "No, I don't think he is. And I think that's OK."

I throw myself at Adam and he slowly lowers me to the floor on my back.

I feel so relaxed like the floor is swallowing me up. Everything spins when I close my eyes. I don't feel my lips anymore. Or Adam's.

Somewhere I hear someone calling my name.

"Min. Minnie!"

I can't open my eyes. They're stuck. I smack my tongue against the roof of my mouth. Fuck! It feels like somebody poured Tidy Cats in there. Tastes about that good, too.

"Hey, Minnie! Wake up."

"What happened?"

"I don't know. One minute I swear we were about to hook up and the next, I'm asleep, half on the futon and you're on your side on the floor in a puddle of drool."

I can only be grateful the puddle of drool is not vomit, because I wouldn't be surprised if it was.

"Well, that's fucking depressing. What a waste of a good drunk."

"Can you really say it was a good drunk if all we did was kiss a little and then pass out."

"I guess not. Adam, I don't think this is ever gonna happen." I wave my index finger flaccidly back and forth between us.

Adam nods in defeat. "I think you're right, Min. Better just *stay friends… and drinking buddies."*

Mimicking Adam's moves from the night before, I manage to crawl to his bathroom and somehow scale the toilet and pee. My head throbs, but I won't allow myself to whine about it because, really, I deserve this pain. I, for all intents and purposes, invited it to replace the pain in my heart. Really I should be grateful for it. It's the distraction I need.

In the midst of admonishing myself, a torrential wave of nausea hits, and I spin my naked ass off the toilet and onto the floor just in time to vomit, splattering puke into the bowl. The splash back hits my face and gets in my hair.

I have no choice but to hop in the shower. The water feels so good on my face and in my tangled, matted, vomitrocious hair. My headache is almost gone. With an asston of caffeine and some McDonald's french fries, I could be good as new by five o'clock tonight.

Adam has coffee waiting for me when I finally emerge from his bathroom. I had no choice but to redress in the Sith Lord outfit I'd sported for the wedding.

He hands me a mug. "Feel any better?"

"I puked."

Adam raises an eyebrow and smirks. "I heard."

"Sorry. I cleaned it up"

"Thanks, probably the first and last time that toilet's ever been cleaned."

My stomach roils at the thought. "Don't tell me that, or I may need to hurl again." I sip the cup of coffee and then have another before announcing that I need to leave.

Adam puts a hand on my shoulder. "Minnie, I'm serious. I

could use some help on the wedding story." As much as I hate to think about it for one more second, I did promise. I know I can get some details out of Clip and Sid that we can use to write the article.

"Let me talk to my brothers and I'll e-mail you tonight. I really gotta get home." My headache is seriously considering returning. I just want to be miserable and wretched by myself in my own bed.

"Let me walk you to the train," Adam says.

I concede.

***

Adam's apartment is around the corner from the train station and SNACKS. The minute we arrive in the courtyard, I turn to look at the café. My favorite place in the world is suddenly not so much my favorite anymore. Through the window of SNACKS, I can see people: my people. My family and Snack's. And his new family—Megan. They must be having a day after the wedding brunch. Those have become very popular. I should know because I've been to a few since "the wedding phase" of my life started—the phase where every other weekend there's a damn wedding. Turning away from the festivities, I grab Adam's arm and pull him so we can get into the train station and out of sight, but I'm too late.

A voice I've known most of my life calls out from across the street. "Minnie!"

Busted! By my baby brother, Sid, during my pseudo walk of shame. Shit!

I turn and wave. I'm sure unnecessary guilt is written across *my face.*

Sid whistles. "You look rough, man!"

"Long night," I explain tersely.

"You were in town and didn't tell anyone?" Sid questions me with a tinge of anger becoming evident in his voice. I nod. He thumbs at Adam. "With this guy?"

"This guy is Adam. He's my new... writing partner," I say defensively.

Sid pulls me away from Adam and whispers in my ear, "OK, well. Snack saw you through the window. Wanted me to come check on you."

I rub my hand up and down one of Sid's arms, force a smile with my lips tight together, and shake my head. "Sid, tell him I'm fine. I'm always fine. Tell him don't forget the Christmas cards. Even though he's married he can still do that."

Sid is utterly confused as I hug him tight. "What?"

I keep holding him. "Just say that to him. He'll understand."

***

Sophia Marie Snackenberg was born May 22, 2006. The birth announcement said they were going to call her Fifi. In the corner right below where Snack signed it were the letters NBU.

Chapter 18
2014 – Sleepover of Shame

Colette, along with the pastries that Snack and I consumed as a midnight dessert, kindly left some casual clothes in the loft. Snack must have told her that he was bringing me here last night, and she took it upon herself to make sure I didn't appear for a second morning in the clothes I went out in the night before.

This time, Snack and I emerge from the loft together. Hand-in-hand.

Dad and Colette are behind the counter with their arms around each other. Colette looks over Dad's shoulder and waves.

My dad turns his head and lifts his chin. "Hey, look who's here, kids. Just in time for brunch."

We're greeted by Aiden and Wookiee. They bounce up and down happily at our appearance. "Daddy! Minnie!"

Wookiee barks repeatedly and weaves figure eights around our legs. I pick him up and my fur boy covers my face with wet puppy kisses.

Dad warns Snack. "You better watch out. That dog is some serious competition for her affection."

"Dad!"

Snack wraps an arm around me. "As long as he's the only competition, I think I can handle it." He kisses Wookiee on the head and then me.

Pictures of Henry crowd my mind.

I get a grateful reprieve from my thoughts when Fifi tugs on my arm. "Did you and Daddy have a sleepover?"

If I recall, sleepovers are a pretty big deal when you're seven. I look to Snack for guidance with how to respond.

Snack throws his head back with a hearty guffaw. "Just go with it!"

I bend down to her level. "Yes, yes we did. That's why we asked you to babysit Wookiee."

Fifi runs over and gives Snack a hug. "Are you happy, Daddy? Your face isn't so sad anymore.

"Yes, Fifi, I am."

"When are you having another sleepover?"

Every time I hear the word 'sleepover' I can only picture the reflection of Snack and me tangled up together in the mirror. It's a little disturbing to be visualizing while talking to a kid.

I glance at Snack, my eyebrows raised in hope. "Soon I hope."

Fifi throws her arms around my waist. "Minnie, you can have a sleepover with Daddy anytime. I'll watch Wookiee whenever you want."

Snack whispers in my ear, "I think we should schedule the next one right away."

Fifi has no idea what she's just given permission for. This kid is actually a cock *unblocker*.

Snack's words have me practically melting. I'd like to run back up to the loft and "sleepover" again.

Fifi looks up at me with her big eyes. "Soon," I tell her. She claps her hands and goes to play with Wookiee.

I push up on my toes and kiss Snack. "Very Soon."

He growls under his breath and we share a knowing grin.

"Now get me coffee."

"Yes, ma'am," he says.

All this frenetic family energy first thing in the morning before my first cup of coffee is overwhelming but I love it. My mind begins to wander, fantasizing what it would be like to wake up to this every day instead of the pristine quiet of my apartment.

Our brunch with my dad, Snack's mom, the kids, and Wookiee is a thing straight out of a television show. The picture-perfect blended family happy and comfortable with each other is something I wish would never end.

***

I need to do a little more packing at my Dad's house, and Snack is going to spend the day with the kids. He convinces me to stay in Downers Grove a bit longer. He wants to take me out again tonight. After checking my upcoming deadlines, I agree, but let him know I need to go back first thing Monday morning.

I can't tell him, but there *is* another reason I need to get back to the city. I need to talk to Henry. I need to see if finding my way back to Snack has been the best thing to ever happen to me or if I've made a spectacular mistake. The way I see it now the former is true. I never considered myself a dishonest person, and Henry and I have never even discussed commitment. Knowing how Snack feels about cheating since he was none too shy about his feelings about his Dad's infidelity, I want whatever this thing I have with Henry settled before I talk to Snack about any sort of future we can have.

***

I'm trying on shoes and figuring out what to wear on my date tonight with Snack when the doorbell rings. It's a little too early for Snack to be here. He isn't supposed to pick me up for another two hours.

Wearing one pair of pumps and holding another in my hands, I go down the stairs and peek out one of the windows beside the door. It *is* Snack. I don't even get the door all the way open when Snack shoves the door open with purpose.

"Hi, you."

I shake my head at the gorgeous, overzealous, and overly punctual man in front of me. "Hi!"

He pins me with my back up against the door. "All I could think about all day was you—the way you looked this morning in the mirror, wearing nothing but me."

His words alone have my thighs heating, my core firing. His hands in my hair and his eyes on face and lips cause me to moan. "Me, too." Snack could easily take me up against this door without complaint from me. "You're early."

"Like I said, I couldn't wait."

"I'm not even dressed."

"Even better."

I push his toward the stairs. Climbing up the stairs behind him, I'm in a very advantageous position to take in an eyeful of his tight, round ass perfectly defined in his jeans.

When we get back to my bedroom I ask, "Well, what do you think? Black or nude?" I hold up the black shoes in my hand and seductively model the nude ones on my feet. Snack doesn't respond. He stands across the room staring at me. He trails his eyes from my feet up my body. Maybe he didn't hear me.

"Snack? Which ones?"

Snack prowls toward me. "Uh… what? I got distracted after you said nude."

Oh. My. God. He's incorrigible! I throw one of the black shoes at him. He catches it, tosses it to the side, and then charges toward me.

He's practically growling as he tells me, "They're nice shoes. I wonder what they'd look like as earrings."

In a whirlwind of motion, Snack swoops me up off my feet, throws me on the bed and stands over me.

He takes one of my legs and pushes it up until my foot is by my ears. He does the same with my other leg. I laugh throughout this imposed yoga session until he lowers himself and grinds his hardened jean-covered cock into my now damp panties. I rock against the roughness of his jeans.

"There, now your shoes are earrings. And I can pound them off you."

Snack just went from zero to naughty in less than two milliseconds. I may swear like a sailor, but that was just filthy and makes me want to come on the spot.

"We need to do something about this panty issue." Snack kisses and sucks my collarbone while rocking against me. He snaps the elastic on the leg of my panties, which only encourages me to grind more. "But I don't want you to move those legs."

Barely breaking our scorching contact, Snack grabs a handful of lace and rapidly rips my midnight blue panties from my ass, tossing them over my head. I watch the whole thing in amazement and delight.

I'm soon without my big sweater, and can't quite figure out how he got it off *and* managed to slip out of his jeans, boxers, and T-shirt while my shoes are still on and up by my head. Could've been all the distracting nibbling of my breasts and stomach. However he did it, I don't care. Snack is working my body and managing my growing need with precision. He's doing all the right things to bring me to the point of screaming. I just want to touch him. I slip my hand around his throbbing and ample hardness and circle my thumb over the crest of his head. It's plush and I swear I sense minute pulses under my palm. Just holding him and touching him shreds to bits any control I'm maintaining.

Snack moans. "Yes!"

It's evident he's only barely in control also.

I guide him into me not caring that he, *we* haven't even

thought about using a condom. Right now I don't care. Snack fills me completely. Just as he said he would, he pounds into me, punishing my G-spot and pressing my clit with his thumb. The unrelenting contract and release of my orgasm sends waves of pleasure from my core and I shake all over. All control has officially been lost.

Snack bellows my name and lets his release go. It's beautiful to see him let loose and relax, sated. Snack drops his head to the space between my shoulder and neck, nuzzling me. "Nude, most definitely the nude."

I laugh aloud. With Snack still seated in me it causes a few more light contractions and one final wave of ecstasy.

I guess he *was* listening.

***

Snuggled next to Snack, I mesh my fingers with his. I can detect his ring indentation on the third finger of his left hand.

"Where's your wedding band?"

Snack is quiet for several moments. I'm about to repeat the question, when he pulls his hand away. He rests it on his rippled abdomen with a smacking sound, almost as if he's spanking himself, punishing himself. "You don't want to hear this."

"Yes, I do." I tell him and sit up next to him, taking his hand back. I run my other hand over the place where he hit himself to soothe it. "I really do."

Snack pushes himself up in the bed until he's sitting with his back against the headboard. We're face-to-face and naked. I don't believe it would be possible to be any more exposed.

In a raw and pained voice, Snack paints a tragic picture. "I took it off and gave it to Megan in the hospital right before she died." He swallows a few times and drops his gaze from my face to our hands. "I slipped it on her thumb and then they started turning off all the machines and she…" Snack's voice tightens and practically disappears. I squeeze his hand gently and he looks up at me with red-rimmed eyes. "She squeezed my hand. Just like what you're doing. It was probably just a reflex or something." He pauses a long time, exhales. "And then she was gone."

Running my thumb across his cheek to catch the lone tear that just fell, I say, "That's messed up."

"Yeah, we had a lot of talks toward the end. Long talks. About how I was supposed to keep going? Be happy. Find love. Believe it or not, she even mentioned you. I think she knew how I felt about you. She even told me not to feel bad about that. What a request." Snack replies as he wipes the back of his hand over his eyes before any more unwanted liquid escapes.

"She was a pretty remarkable person." I say with full honesty. Even from the grave just as she had in life, Megan was being kind to me. She was giving Snack back to me.

"Minnie, what I told you last night? It's true. I was scared to move it to another level with you for fear of losing you forever. Of being hurt. But it was more than that. Your brother constantly telling me not to hurt you, it really stuck. I never wanted to hurt you."

I take Snack's other hand in mine. "I know that now."

"I tried to duplicate the connection we had with my... with Megan, but I couldn't."

I completely understand about trying to make another relationship feel like what I felt when I'm with Snack. Isn't that what I've been searching for? Trying to do with Henry? And failing miserably. This conversation hits a little too close to home. "So, you kept me on the reserve list. You wanted to make sure you had a deep bench!"

Snack smiles and laughs, a strained laugh, full of suppressed emotion, but still a laugh. He pulls my hands toward him. "Look at you! Using a sports analogy."

"I've lived my whole life around men. I know sports," I pronounce defensively. The thing is I'm *not* lying. I still *do* live with men. Well, *man*. Henry's face flashes in my mind. I really need to tell Snack about him. Or do I? If I'm going to end it with Henry tomorrow, why should I tell Snack? Wouldn't it just hurt him? I dismiss the internal debate and refocus on Snack.

"No, you're not on the bench. I... I'm pretty sure you're my closer."

"Closer?" Honestly, I really didn't know that much about sports.

"Jeez, Minnie. You know as much about sports as I do about Star Wars. The pitcher that closes the game. Brings it all home. Wins. *That's* the closer."

Throwing a leg over Snack, I straddle him his lap. "Are we talking about football or baseball?"

Snack releases my hands and places his on my hips,

tracing circles with his thumbs around my hipbones. "We aren't talking about sports at all. We are talking about us."

"I'm so confused right now. I don't know if I should be offended or flattered."

Snack chuckles. He encircles my waist with one arm, dragging me up his body. "Flattered. Always flattered. You always said, 'If we break up—that's it!' That's why I always said we weren't. NBU, never broken up. Because the game, our game, our love, it never ended, and you're going to win it for us. My closer. My girl."

Did Snack just say in a roundabout way that he loved me?

Leaning in closely, I hold his face in my hands and with my eyes look deep into the blueness and wordlessly communicate, as clearly as I can, that he's a wonderful man.

Wookiee marches up the length of the bed and settles right by Snack's hand. He makes a soft low growl. Snack ruffles the fur on the top of Wookiee's head. "Don't worry buddy. I'd never hurt your mommy."

So says he. I'm now so crazy about Snack, I'm in more danger of being hurt than ever before.

Chapter 19
2014 – Back home in Chicago

Snack dropped Wookiee and me off at the train station. I told him not to stay with me until the train came. It would only make it more difficult to leave. He kissed me hard like he was marking his claim and then more softly to show me how much he cared. When he stopped, he whispered, "I love you."

He said he loved me! At that moment, I'm pretty sure a full Fourth of July fireworks display along with accompaniment by The London Symphony Orchestra directed by John Williams went off. I was out of my mind with happiness. Snack loves me!

I giggled and channeled Han Solo like he did all those years ago. "I know."

Snack smirked. "I deserved that."

Resting my head on Snack's shoulder, I sigh.

"Even right now, as happy as I am, I'm so afraid it will happen again. Something bad. I'm afraid I'll lose you. How can I deserve you after passing you over not once but twice?"

Picking up my head and twisting in the seat to face him fully, I kiss Snack one more time. "You know I can't promise that it won't, but I'll do every thing in my power to make sure it doesn't. I'm gonna miss you."

Snack kisses me gently and whispers, "I don't want to have time to miss you. I'll see you soon... real soon!"

The train journey back into the city was like waking up from a dream. The closer I got to the city, the more I was conscious of the unpleasant task ahead of me.

***

When I finally return home after my extended weekend with Snack, I'm not greeted at the door. No, Henry is sitting on the sofa, drinking what I'm sure is a some pretentious artisanal craft beer out of a pint glass, tapping away on his laptop, and watching an episode of something on the Esquire Network.

He barely looks up when I enter. "Welcome back. Why'd you stay in Downers Grove for so long?"

I don't expect him to be so direct, but I'm not sensing he's angry. He still isn't giving me his full attention. Actually he's acting like its just any old late afternoon and I haven't been away from him for almost four days.

"Uh, I hung out with an old friend."

"An old friend?"

"Yeah. Marcus Snackenburg."

"Snack?"

"Yeah."

"Well, I'd say he's more than an old friend, wouldn't you?" He has finally stopped typing and watches me take off my coat and put away my things.

"Uh… yeah," I mumble and turn away, pretending to dig for something in my purse. Oh my God, he knows! How could he possibly know? How guilty am I? I live in the Midwest, but right now I'm far away, lying on a beach of guilt with grains of sand made of guilt. Water comprised of guilt laps at my toes. When things can't get much worse, a giant saltwater wave of guilt crashes down unexpectedly, waterboarding me with guilt. I *should* be feeling guilt. In this moment all I have is guilt. All the guilt I was actively ignoring all weekend.

"He's your best friend, right?" Henry shrugs.

Oh, thank God. He doesn't know. I have to tell him. I can't wait. That would be wrong. Or is it? Because, well, Snack didn't really say we were going to *be* something. The last thing he said before I got on the train home was that he would see me soon… *real soon*. That's not the promise of a future. Not that I have or really want any kind of promise from Henry, either.

Henry has continued talking while my brain—and my heart, if I'm telling the truth—is back with Snack in the loft above the café, reliving our sleepover.

"I figured he was, considering all those stories you told me about when you were kids."

As I walk by the couch, Henry reaches up and pulls me down for a peck on the lips. Wookiee growls loudly from my purse at him in protest. The kiss is automatic, dictated behavior without meaning. It's clear to me, I don't feel for Henry the way I do for Snack. Still, I am in some sort of relationship with him.

"Yes. He's my best friend."

Wookiee sounds his exception to my statement in a low, huffy bark.

"Oh sorry, buddy." I pluck Wookiee out and nuzzle him in apology. He licks me in acceptance. "And you! You little monkey-faced fur boy, you're my bestest, best friend."

Henry lost interest as soon as I geared my attention to Wookiee and is back at his laptop. "Well, glad you're back. I even missed the tiny terrorist."

Wookiee, again, growls deeply at Henry when he makes eye contact.

Henry pays no attention. He never does. And then he abruptly changes the subject. "Wanna fuck later? It's been awhile."

Wanna fuck? Is that really how we talk to each other? Is that really what I was OK with? It used to be a turn on. Now it just feels… gross.

"Maybe," I say evasively. "I'm kinda tired."

"OK, whatever."

I'm perfectly fine, really relieved at his response. I think I have my answer to my dilemma because "OK, whatever" is not the response of someone who's been missing you. For someone in love, being perfectly OK with "OK, whatever" isn't, either.

Chapter 20
2014 – Too Soon

As much as I wanted to call or text Snack after I left Downers Grove, I didn't. I wanted everything to be settled with Henry before I communicated with him again. I didn't want anything potentially in our way. Snack didn't contact me, either. My hope is that he was missing me, but giving me space. I vowed to myself I would text him right after I talked to Henry tonight after work. It would be a little more than twenty-four hours since I last saw Snack. That wasn't too long.

I couldn't concentrate at work. Managing to write five paragraphs about my latest assignment took all day. My heart wasn't in it and my brain kept playing back visions of my weekend with Snack, while simultaneously trying to piece together the words to end things with Henry.

Entering my apartment, I throw my purse and phone on the bar in the kitchen, scoop up Wookiee to give him a kiss, and then head to the bathroom.

The lights are sort of low in the place, but there's enough light coming in that I don't think to turn on a light. And I *really* have to pee after my long ride on the 'L' from downtown Chicago to Hyde Park. Henry must not be home. I don't even yell out for him, because secretly I'm happy for a few more moments to think before I have to talk to him.

Wookiee barks at the bathroom door as I wash my hands. I run my hands through my hair and quickly brush my teeth. I check my watch: 4:36. Henry must be home.

Looking in the mirror I give myself a little pep talk. "Come on, Minnie! Since when have you been such a wimp? Get your fucking act together. If you want to be with Snack then you have to let something go. And really, what are you letting go? You know you don't love Henry."

I nod once and then turn, open the door, and stride through with conviction.

The room is even darker, but now there is the soft glow of candlelight all around and music playing. Henry pops up from behind the bar in the kitchen with a roasting pan in his oven-mitted hands.

"Good, you're finally out."

What the fuck! What's going on? Romance? Candles? Has Henry been knocked on his head?

"Wow," I say.

Henry places the pan on the bar and yanks off the oven mitts, dropping them on a barstool as he passes.

"I wanted to surprise you." Henry motions to our small dining room table. It's set with my nicest dishes and flatware, cloth napkins, candles, and flowers.

I shake my head in confusion. "Well, I'm definitely surprised." It's going to be so much harder to tell Henry what I need to tell him now that he's gone and done this. "What's this all about?"

Henry comes right up to me. He takes a piece of my hair that has fallen in my face and tucks in behind my ear. Then he takes both my hands. The mood in the room shifts from surreal to serious.

"Minnie," Henry says and straightens his back. "We've been together for what… eight, nine months? I like you. We work, ya know? You do your thing, I do mine and then we have really hot sex. And well, I think that's a pretty major thing, too. I think I missed you this weekend. I've never really missed you before, so I was thinking maybe we could…" Henry lets go of one of my hands and reaches into his back pocket.

There is an insistent knock on the door of the apartment. Henry tries to ignore it.

"I was thinking maybe we could…" More knocking. "God dammit!" He stomps off to the door and throws it open. I can't see who it is because Henry's blocking my view. "What do you want?"

"Is, uh, Minnie here?" Oh, no. It's Snack.

"Yeah, who are you?"

"I'm Snack."

"Snack, oh, man, good to meet you. It's kind of not a good time."

I hear Snack ask, "Who are *you*?

I run to the door and arrive just in time to hear Henry declare, "I'm Minnie's boyfriend. She's my girl."

In unison, Snack and I say, "What?" both with disbelief and anger.

I look down at Henry's hand and see a black velvet ring box opened with a shiny ring sitting on a pillow of white satin.

My mind spins. Fucking Henry. And what the hell is Snack doing here?

"Snack, what are you doing here?"

Snack's voice is tight, emotionless. "I got your address from your dad. I texted you. Didn't you get it?"

"No, I haven't looked at my phone since I got home." I pat my pockets and then turn my head and look over at the bar. "Where's my phone?"

Snack lifts his phone up, types something and Henry's pocket lights up. He has my phone! He pulls it out and hands it to me. I snatch it from his hand, the anger boiling in my gut. "You took it? You were hiding it?"

"It was on the bar. I saw you had a message from Snack."

I look at the message.

IS IT TOO SOON for SOON?
Coming to get you, right now!

As I read it, Henry keeps talking. "It only convinced me I needed to ask you sooner rather than later."

Snack snaps at Henry. "Ask her what? To marry her? Minnie, what's happening? What about last weekend?"

"It's not what you think, Snack," I say.

"Yeah, I was," Henry adds. "What the fuck happened last weekend?"

Wookiee interjects into the verbal spar, barking at Snack and growling at Henry while jumping and running around their feet.

I hold up a finger. "Wait, just wait"—I look at Henry—"'I'm her boyfriend?'

Fuck! Seriously, Henry? That word has never, *ever* escaped your lips before today. What are you thinking? My girl? I was never your girl. What's gotten into you?"

When I spin around from unloading on Henry, Snack is gone.

"Snack?" I yell down the hallway. The hallway is quiet and he's nowhere to be seen. A few of the neighbors opened their doors a crack to see what's going on.

I snap at them, "Mind your own fucking business!" Wookiee is no longer barking. Where is he?

I shove past a dumbstruck Henry and survey the apartment. Wookiee is nowhere in sight! He must have followed Snack down the hall. I can only hope he didn't get into the elevator.

I run down the hall. No Wookiee. He must be to the ground floor by now. Hopefully, Snack picked him up and will bring him back. I charge down the seven flights of stairs to try and catch the elevator carrying the two most important men in my life.

When I reach the ground floor, there's nobody in the lobby. As I exit the building, I hear screeching tires and see Snack's Honda Odyssey pulling away from the curb, but no

Wookiee… until there is an audible thump and a squealing cry of pain behind me. I turn my head away from Snack's vehicle just at the moment Wookiee's body flies in the air and drops with an awful smack against the curb. I roar like a howler monkey! The motorcycle that just hit him buzzes away and I scream.

"Wookiee!" I run to the curb and fall to my knees; I can already hear his pitiful whines. He's obviously hurt, but thankfully appears conscious. His breathing is shallow and one of his front paws is off at a strange angle. His little body so still. The terror in his eyes is heartbreaking. He's so scared. I don't know what to do. Is it safe to move him?

"Wookiee, monkey puppy. I'm here. It's going to be OK." I stroke his ears and run the back of my hand down this face. I'm afraid to touch him too much, but I need him to know I'm here. "I love you. I love you so much, Wookiee." My vision is blurring with tears.

I feel someone hovering behind me and can make out Henry's voice. I have no sense of what he's saying.

Wookiee vomits blood and as it trickles to the ground, his eyes close. There is not a moment to waste. I scoop Wookiee up next to my chest, jump to my feet, and yell at Henry to get the car. I only hope I haven't injured him further, but I can't just stay here and watch him die.

I feel Wookiee's ribs gently and can make out that he's still breathing, but not deeply. Even though his eyes are closed, he whines softly and I loosen my grip.

Henry calls the vet and once they answer he lets them know we're coming in emergently.

I can't breathe. I can't think. I can't imagine a life without Wookiee. And I don't want to.

It's altogether possible that I was out and in the vet's office before Henry even stopped the car. All I know is we were greeted at the door by a tech that gathered up Wookiee.

"Give us a minute. We'll be right out to get you," she says.

I thrust my hands through my hair and fall to the floor of the reception area. I look down to see the front of my tunic top covered in Wookiee's blood, my leggings ripped and wet from the snow. I sensed myself being lifted and then being seated in a chair, but I would never have been able to tell you how or who got me there.

"Minnie?"

My head is buried in my hands and I squeeze my eyes shut. When I finally open them, a pair of familiar shoes are in my view. I don't want to talk to him. If we hadn't fought over him calling me his girlfriend, we wouldn't be here.

I don't look up at Henry. "Your shit needs to be out of my apartment by the time I get back. Do you hear me? Leave!"

Henry starts crying. "What about Wookiee?"

Now? Now is when he finally shows some emotion. I can't even look at Henry. I just shake my head. "He's none of your concern."

"Please let me stay here with you," Henry squats down in front of me. He reaches his hand out toward my knee, but when I flinch, he pulls it back.

"Why?" I raise my head and spit at him. Then I stand,

wobbling on my feet. "What could you possibly do for me? Or for Wookiee? If you hadn't taken my phone or planned that fucking proposal, Wookiee wouldn't have gotten hurt. Leave, Henry, now!"

"If you hadn't fucked Snack, we wouldn't be here either!" He's right.

I collapse back in the chair and cover my eyes with my hands. Through heaving sobs I say, "Don't think I haven't thought that." When I finally look up, Henry is gone.

It's more than an hour later when the vet comes out to talk to me. I've been antagonizing the techs at the desk every ten minutes. They have been so patient with me.

The doctor ushers me to a small consultation room. "Ms. Cooper, I'm Dr. Gerard. Wookiee is stable."

I finally exhale all the anxiety I've been holding since Wookiee was hit. A long sobbing breath escapes my mouth. "Thank God."

Dr. Gerard continues, "Critical, but stable. He has several broken ribs, a punctured lung and two broken legs that will have to be surgically repaired. We need to discuss what to do next."

There is no question about what should be done, and I tell the doctor just that, "Do everything. Anything. Do whatever you need to do to make him better."

Dr. Gerard lifts his eyebrows and cocks his head. "He's badly injured. The next twenty-four hours are critical. It will be a long recovery. It could be quite expensive."

"I don't care."

When I ask if I can see him, I'm told Wookiee is sedated.

I can see him when he wakes up, but right now they are keeping him comfortable and monitoring his breathing because of his lung. The vets and all the techs implore me to go home, but I don't. The clinic is open twenty-four hours a day. Even if I can't see Wookiee, I want to be here when he wakes up, so I sleep sitting up on the hard chairs in the waiting room.

***

I wake to the sun streaming through the windows in the waiting room. Fucking happy sun! It's pissing me off. Everything is making me mad. The weather refusing to spontaneously reflect my mood is just piling on. God, I can't breathe. Even though Wookiee is out of the woods, the sadness in my heart and the fucking inherent happiness of beautiful day are choking me. There needs to be a fucking hurricane outside. That would be the only appropriate meteorological response to what lives in me right now.

Fuck, Henry! Fuck his stupid proposal and his stupid fucking too late half-assed declaration of affection.

Damn, Snack! Why did he run away? If he'd just stayed and listened, Wookiee would be fine!

Even though I'm mad at everything and everyone, I'm particularly pissed at myself. All my plans and dreams shot to hell. I cheated on Henry. I lied to Snack. And Wookiee! I've focused so much energy on Snack and my stupid unrequited love for him for so long that I neglected to see I've been living with the man of my dreams all along.

Wookiee.

My eight-inch tall stud muffin.

Some fucking luck I have—I'm in love with a man I'm sure I'll never have and a little man I could lose.

I look around the waiting room. I'm the only one here. Checking the time on my phone I see it's quarter to seven. I never would've slept this late if I were at home. With Wookiee. I would've been up an hour ago for our morning walk. If Wookiee was OK. A sudden involuntary sob escapes my lungs.

I look at my phone again. Two texts. One from Henry.

I have all my essentials out. I'll have to have the rest of my stuff picked up. How's Wookiee? I know we never got along well, but I would never want him to be hurt. Please let me know. About Wookiee.
And when I can pick up my things.

And the one from Snack I never got to answer.

IS IT TOO SOON for SOON?
Coming to get you, right now!

I begin to sob even harder, trying to decide which text to respond to first. I decide to text Snack, but then a vet tech approaches and places a hand gently on my shoulder. "Ms. Cooper, Dr. Gerard left instructions after the surgery last night to bring you back to see Wookiee as soon as he came out of sedation."

I'm surprised and pleased the doctor stayed and operated. I jump up from my seat. "He's awake?"

"Yes," the tech says. "He's awake but still pretty wonky. He's also got a paralytic onboard and he's intubated. When he sees you he'll probably try to move. Don't encourage him."

I nod and she ushers me to the back. I spot Wookiee the minute I walk through the doors to the recovery area, but I'm scared to move toward him. Even this far away I can see the tube taped to his mouth and a large lime green cast on his back leg.

"It's OK to go closer." The tech placed a hand on my arm.

"I'm scared."

"It's going to be OK. Wookiee's a strong boy."

With each step my heart breaks. It's not only his back leg that has a cast, but the front one that was bent badly also. There are huge patches of fur shaved away near his ribs, which are wrapped and have a tube coming out of them, on both his casted legs all the way up to the shoulder, and on his other front leg where he has an IV. The tech explains all the tubes and stuff, and as she does, Wookiee opens his eyes. The scared look is gone, and he acknowledges me with a drunken stare and an almost inaudible whimper

The tech was right. Wookiee tries to move. He lifts his head but I tell him in a tear-filled whisper, "Hi, Wook. Hi, my brave boy. Don't move. I'm here… I'm—" I can't stop the sobs. I turn to the tech. "Can I kiss him on the head?"

"Yes, gently."

I kiss him right between the eyes and he closes them and lowers his head with a sigh. He's so still. Too still. I glance, panicked, at the tech.

She looks up at a monitor. "He's fine. He's just sleeping."

I look down at my precious fur boy and hold my hand to my chest. I hope I'm making the right decision. Right now, I don't know. He looks so bad. Am I being selfish, making him stay? But then again, his coming through the surgery has to mean something.

"Ms. Cooper," the nurse interrupts my internal struggle. "Wookiee is going to need to rest today—all day. You look like you could use some rest, too." I start to argue, but she just continues and points at my bloodied shirt. "And maybe a shower and fresh clothes. They won't let you in to see him again until he's more awake and drinking on his own." After several more refusals to leave, I submit, but only after I'm assured that I can be with Wookiee the second it's OK and that everyone working for the next day has my cell number.

***

I scowl at the table still set for Henry's proposal and head to the bathroom. I promptly curl up in a ball in the tub with a bottle of Absolut Citron I nabbed from the freezer on the way in. I look at my phone, wishing for a call telling me Wookiee has made a miraculous recovery. No such luck. Only the two texts from Henry and Snack that I have no interest in returning right now. I drink until I sleep, which doesn't take much.

When I wake, the first thing I do is scramble for the phone; afraid I've slept through a call. Still nothing. I've slept in the tub for four hours. Feeling not quite in my body and perhaps a bit hung over, I take another drink straight from the bottle, get out of the tub, and turn on the water for a shower. I strip out of my clothes robotically and get in the shower reluctantly. I'm scared to be away from my phone for even a few minutes. I shower quickly, taking care of just the very necessities. No lingering over shaving and primping. Wash, rinse, out. As if that will make the phone ring. When I get out, I'm again disappointed. No message. I turn the ringer up to the loudest setting, just in case, and throw on a pair of yoga pants, my Middlebury sweatshirt, and thick socks. I thoughtlessly rake a comb through my hair and leave it wet.

Little did I know that I would repeat this routine at home for four more days between visits to the vet's office. Every day I go, another tube is gone. First, the breathing tube, then the chest tube, and finally the IV. Once Wookiee can eat and drink on his own and tolerate being on his feet for brief periods, they allow me to take him home. I had already called in that I would be out and working from home until further notice. Thank God for my backlog of unused articles. With a bit of fluffing I'm able to shoot two to my editor without much effort.

Taking Wookiee home was bittersweet and full of surprises. The first was when I went to pay the bill, which I had told would be estimated at five to eight thousand dollars. I was told it was paid in full. This had to be a mistake and I told the girl at the desk as much, but she insisted. I shook my head in disbelief and gratitude. It could've only been one person—Henry.

The second I knew for sure was when I carried Wookiee into the apartment to find every trace of Henry gone. He must have figured out when Wookiee was getting out without me telling him and arranged to get the rest of his things while I was out. Very considerate. Very un-Henry.

Maybe the next girl he's with will benefit from our unfortunate relationship. On the kitchen bar is an envelope with his keys and no note. After settling Wookiee in a nest of blankets on the sofa, I fish my phone out of my bag and send Henry a two-word text to which he replied:

You're welcome. It's the least I could do.

Now, there's only Snack left to talk to, but I'm not ready. I don't know what to say yet. All I can focus on is Wookiee. Getting myself dressed, staying a little buzzed at all times, and Wookiee. Maybe in a few days.

Chapter 21
2014 – Sid and Clip to the Rescue

Nine days have lapsed since Wookiee's accident. I won't leave his side even to take a shower. The few I have managed since he's been home have been cursory and with his makeshift dog bed transferred to the bathroom. I have to look out of the curtain every seconds or so to make sure he's still there. Which is stupid because he isn't moving very quickly, nor does he want to be away from me. Wookiee just cocks his head and looks up at me each time he hears the scraping of the shower hooks against the rod. I perceive the look on his sweet face to be somewhere between exhaustion and "I think my mom's gone crazy."

While drying myself, I hear the front door open. It can't be Henry. He left his key. My super? Why wouldn't he knock before letting himself in? I dry quickly and throw on the dirty sweatshirt and yoga pants I just took off. Wookiee perks up his ears, but strangely doesn't bark. He's been pretty quiet since coming home.

I creep out in the small hallway between my bedroom and bathroom and hear familiar voices.

Sid says, "Well, where do you think she is?"

Clip pokes around some of my mail on the counter. "I don't—"

"I'm right here, assholes! Why are you breaking into my apartment?"

Clip, after a big sigh of relief, rushes toward me and hugs me. "Oh, right, we're the assholes. Where the fuck have you been? Dad hasn't heard from you since you left over a week ago. Nobody has been able to get ahold of you. Snack is acting like a fucking lunatic."

"I've been a little busy."

"Too busy to communicate with anyone?

As if on cue, Wookiee hobbles out from the bathroom. After one look, Clip and Sid drop to their knees to greet him.

"Holy fuck!" Sid pets Wook's head.

"Min, What happened? What the fuck happened to Wook?" Clip pipes in.

I calmly point to Wookiee as he shivers and finally plants himself awkwardly in a modified sit before them. "That's what I've been doing."

We sit on the floor while I retell the entire story of Wookiee's accident, not leaving anything out.

Clip reaches over and squeezes my arm and Sid puts one arm around me while patting Wook on the head. I allow myself the small comfort of resting my head on my much bigger little brother's shoulder. I have to swipe away the stream of tears that run down my cheeks. It's hard to relive

Wookiee's accident, but the of pain remembering what happened is getting less and less by the day. The room is dark with only a smidgen of light sneaking through the curtains that I've kept drawn. There are empty vodka bottles and cans of SpaghettiOs in the sink and on the bar, along with prescription bottles of Wookiee's medicines and mail piled up. This is not my normal operating procedure.

"God, look at this place!" Clip scolds me. "Look at you! Jesus, you and Snack deserve each other. You are two of the stupidest smart people I know!"

The mention of Snack's name and I fire a line of psycho questioning.

"How is he?"

Why the fuck do I care?

"Never mind. I don't care."

Yes, I want to know. I miss him.

"Wait! How is he?"

"As bad as you, if not worse. He's been drinking a lot, ignoring the kids, staying out late," Sid pipes in. They both get up and start cleaning up my apartment, something I've never seen either of them do without the threat of death from our father. I scoop Wookiee up gently to cuddle him close.

Clip is in the kitchen doing dishes when Sid throws open the curtains and blinds me with the hazy brightness of the winter sun.

I shield my eyes. "Ow!"

Sid puts his hands on his hips. "Shit! Minnie, you look like shit!"

"Thanks!" I bite out sarcastically. "I sort of feel like shit so I'm going for a clothes-match-the-mood vibe."

Clip stacks the last few plates, cans and, yes, vodka bottles on a dishcloth and comes out of the kitchen. "Dude, you fucked up. Snack fucked up. Hell, the mysterious invisible *not boyfriend* fucked up. But you're all still alive. The only one that really got screwed in this deal was Wookiee."

Wookiee whines softly at the mention of his name.

"I think things are really messed up with Snack for good this time," I say, dropping my head in defeat.

Clip kneels in front of me on the floor, reaches out, and picks up my chin so I have to look at him. "Min, he's been in love with you forever. And I know you feel the same."

"You didn't help with that much."

"Yeah, I know. Whatever. You need to figure that shit out. What do *you* want?" Clip raises his eyebrow.

Sid adds, "Because in case you forgot, there's a wedding in our future."

I look back and forth between them. "What? One of you?"

"No, moron. Did you forget? Dad and Colette. Snack's about to become your stepbrother. So no matter what happens with you guys, if you love each other or hate each other, you're going to have to tolerate each other because you're about to be related."

Then Sid whispers to Clip, "One way or another."

Clip drags me to my feet and carefully lifts Wookiee out of my arms and hands him off to Sid. "What the fuck are you doing? Give him back"

"We'll wait here, while you take a shower."

"Fuck you, Clip. I just took one."

My brother grabs my arm and drags me into the bathroom shower. Without releasing my arm he turns on the shower. "Take another one. Use some shampoo. And brush your damn teeth. Jesus, Minnie, it's only three o'clock and you smell like a fucking distillery. Put on some makeup, too, if not for yourself, for me. You're depressing me!"

"What about Wookiee?"

"Don't worry, we'll watch him. You just get yourself together."

Clip's tough brother thing is actually pretty fucking sweet. That and the really hot shower sobers me up quickly.

***

In the taxi, on the way over to Union Station with Clip, Sid, and a carefully packaged-for-transport Wookiee; I call my dad to let him know I'm OK. I have to repeat the happenings of the last week or so yet again. It's actually becoming easier to talk about the accident, and I don't feel like bawling through the whole tale anymore.

My dad listens patiently after his initial relief at hearing my voice. Finally he says, "Snack's been calling. He even came over here and asked me very personal stuff about you. You and Henry."

"What did you say?"

"I told him I'd never met the guy and that you didn't seem serious about him."

"Thanks, Dad."

"Why thanks, it's the truth, right?"

"Yes. I've never been serious about anybody but Snack. I've just been trying to get through life without him since he let me down."

"I know, Mouse."

"How do you know?"

"I'm old, but I'm not deaf, dumb, and stupid. It's pretty fucking obvious. Colette and I have known you have two loved each other for a long time. Still love each other.

I laugh. It feels good. "Nice use of the fuck word, Dad."

***

So, I'm going to Downers Grove. Maybe to say good-bye to the possibility of Snack forever. Or maybe not. Maybe I'll just have another brother?

Living like this. Guarding your heart? Guarding everything like you're afraid the crazy neighbor kid is going to come over and break your toy is killing me. Trust me I've had years to perfect this. I've been living with a condom around my heart to protect myself from love. Guess what? There isn't one. And frankly, I'm ready to be in love without protection. From the little I've experienced, I already know it will feel better.

Chapter 22
2014 – The Love(s) of My Life

The snow is filthy. That is the first thing I notice when we get off the train in Downers Grove. It had lost all of its newness and purity. Sort of the way my renewed relationship with Snack had. I thought it had pureness and potential, but it seems I am wrong. I fucked it up by cheating and lying. He fucked it up by running.

The second thing I notice is Snack. He is walking away from me on the other side of Main Street with a giggling woman running after him. Jacksy, Jennifer Jacksy. The loosest girl that ever went to Downers Grove North High School. When she catches up to him, she throws her arms around him from behind.

Here I am standing in my favorite place. The snow is gross. It's right before twilight when the sun is low and harsh and Snack is walking away. I know he has no idea I'm here, but it just feels too… yucky. Like, once again, our timing is off.

Standing here, holding my injured, exhausted dog—*my injured, exhausted heart gives up*. This can no longer be my favorite place. I have to find a new one, because this one no longer feels like hope.

My brothers flank me sort of like the day we moved to Downers Grove. They see the same thing I do—Snack and Jacksy walking down the street, probably toward Whiskey, Beer, and Barbeque.

I say out loud with resignation, "Fuck it. Forget it."

I turn around to go back into the station to wait for the next train back to the city when Sid sticks his fingers in his mouth and whistles.

Clip yells, "Yo, Snackenberg! Come here!"

Snack's head snaps up, but I can't look. I lower my head and kiss Wookiee on the skull and then slap at them both with my free hand.

I grit my teeth. "God dammit, guys. Just let it go!"

Snack jogs over and before I know it he's in front of us. His scent proceeds him—the unique combination of clean and cinnamon and Snack.

I look everywhere but at his face because I'm afraid of what I'll see in his eyes. Hate. Disappointment. Rejection.

Snack greets my brothers with a nod. It gets quiet. A quiet that goes on too long.

Once again I turn to leave, but a firm hand grasps my shoulder before I've even moved ten degrees.

"Minnie?"

I finally look up. I don't see any of the things I feared I would. Only concern. "What happened? What's wrong with Wookiee?"

Wookiee whimpers and wiggles out of my arms for Snack. I hold Wookiee tighter.

Then for some reason anger boils up in me and instead of telling him about Wookiee's accident, I light into him. "Seriously?" I point across the street. "Jennifer Jacksy?"

My brothers both back away. Cowards.

Snack shrugs in defeat. "She's a 7-11. You know, open all night. Convenient. You can get what you want quickly and go home. It's the place you go when you need something fast, but don't want to make the effort to go to the real store. And I think the *store* I should've shopped in all along is about to close, so I was gonna go to Jacksy. To 7-11."

This conversation is ridiculous and actually a bit comical. I'm somewhere between pissed off and amused as I try not to smile. "Are you fucking comparing me to a grocery store?"

"No, I'm not. I'm comparing Jacksy to a 7-11. It's a joke, Minnie. Nothing happened. Or will happen with Jacksy. And I've never even been close to comparing you to a grocery store." Snack and I stare at each other. I don't know what he's feeling exactly, but I'm happy and angry and confused and all of a sudden hopeful.

Clip and Sid are laughing, looking between us.

Sid says, "You guys are so weird."

Slapping Snack on the arm as he goes, Clip runs off toward the waiting Jacksy. He yells to us over his shoulder, "Ya know what? I was always into Slurpees and those hot dogs on the rollers. I think I'd like some 7-11 right now."

Sid laughs and makes his exit, too. "Uh, I think I hear Colette calling. Yeah, that's definitely Colette." Sid runs into

SNACKS, but Colette is nowhere in sight let alone calling to him.

Snack and I are left alone with Wookiee. I can't control Wookiee's wiggling any longer. Snack plucks him from my arms and I give no resistance. It's literally a relief to have someone else care for him for a moment. I shake my head and allow the giggle I've been suppressing free.

Seeing Snack before me, rubbing Wookiee's ears, and telling him he's so sorry he was hurt; the tornado of emotions swirls up again.

"Tell me what happened... to Wookiee... to us," Snack implores.

We sit on one of the benches in the courtyard of the train station even though the wind is starting to blow a bit harder.

It's the third time I relay Wookiee's tale in one day and this time I do it with only a few sobs. Snack, on the other hand, is a blubbering mess. With each detail he kisses Wookiee and apologizes, or strokes his fur and apologizes. It's touching.

Snack heaves out three large sighs and then asks, "Why didn't you call me? Or text? I could've helped."

I shake my head. Why didn't I call him? I thought he hated me. And to be honest, Snack was part of the reason Wookiee was injured as much as I was. "I started to text you a million times and one emotion or another stopped me. And you ran away."

"It looked like you needed to work things out with that guy."

"Henry."

"Henry. Do you... Do you love him?" Snack makes a move to take my hand, but then at the last minute pulls back and carefully holds the cast on Wookiee's front paw.

After a long pause and contemplating the octagon tiles in the courtyard of the train station for far too long, I say slowly and truthfully, "Snack, I can't love Henry because I've never been out of love with you." Then I spell it out as plainly as possible. "We were fuck buddies." It sounds harsh when I say it. I rephrase. "Friends with Benefits. Although, I don't think I really would've chosen him for a friend. We were just two people that lived together and occasionally did things together and slept together, but there was no true connection, no commitment. There never was and there never will be because its over. And I'm sorry I cheated, but I didn't see it that way—part of me had been cheating on him all along—with you, emotionally."

Snack stands suddenly. "When's the next train?"

Weird question. "Soon. Like six forty-five, I think. The one after that is around eight." I'm confused. Does he want me to go? He hasn't said a thing about what I just told him. He seems agitated—angry, even.

"OK, let's go," Snack says without emotion.

He *does* want me to leave. I swallow the tears running down the back of my throat. "I don't have a ticket yet."

Snack grabs my wrist and firmly, wordlessly implores me to sit back down. I don't understand.

"Minnie, I'm *panicking* inside talking to you here. Like you can escape too easily. What I mean is... let's both leave... go somewhere else."

So he wants me to stay. "Why'd you ask about the train?"

"Because I don't want to say what I need to say, want to say, in a train station full of commuters. Just a sec." Snack holds up one finger, pulls out his phone, and taps out a text.

What is he doing?

Snack reads my thoughts. "I'm finding a quiet place for us."

Wookiee, to the best of his current physical ability, has rolled himself up into a ball in Snack's arms, his eyes closed contently.

Snack stands and locks his tired, but sparkling eyes right into mine. He offers his hand, I take it, and he pulls me up to my feet just in time to glance across the street to observe Sid and Colette getting in Colette's car. Sid doesn't look at us but Colette blows us a little kiss and a wave. Then she appears to look at Snack for a couple of elongated seconds before winking at him.

"She closed early?"

"I told her I needed somewhere private. Besides, Gil will be thrilled to have her home early. They rarely get an entire evening together."

I'm thankful for the space, but it's going to be hard to let Snack go in the middle of SNACKS, if that's what needs to happen. Snack places his hand on the small of my back. I don't move until he applies a little pressure urging me forward.

Chapter 23
2014 – Here We Go Again

We get up to the loft and immediately I want to leave. This is a mistake. This is too much. There are too many memories here.

Snack says plainly, "I've only loved two women in my life."

I walk over to Snack and take Wookiee from his arms. "I can't do this again. I can't be second choice to a ghost again. Charlotte is dead. Megan is dead. I'm alive and I'm still not good enough. I've been in love with you *forever*, Snack. Like forever, forever. Before you were my friend. Before you *liked me* liked me. Before you smashed my heart the first time. But I will not be anyone's second choice. I'm sorry I lied to you. I didn't mean for it to wind up with all of us getting hurt. So, I'm saying good-bye. Good-bye, Snack. Please say good-bye to the kids for me. I promise to keep sending Christmas cards."

Snack takes Wookiee back out of my arms and places

him gently on an armchair by the fire. Wookiee instantly toddles in a circle and makes himself at home by rolling up into a ball. He closes his eyes—tired from today's adventure.

Snack blocks my retreat. "No, you will not send me any more Christmas cards and I won't say good-bye to the kids for you."

"But—"

Snack's voice gets low. "Let me finish. It's true. I've only loved two women in my life, Min—"

"I know, I know. Megan and Char—"

"Just shut the fuck up, Min!" Snack emphasizes every word and yells up toward the rafters. He runs his hands through his hair.

Oh my God, Snack just swore. He never swears. That was my specialty. He always felt it showed a lack of vocabulary. I disagreed. I contend you can use the word fuck most effectively and in many ways.

Snack is everywhere. He can't seem to stop moving around the loft. I stand in the same place, practically paralyzed. He starts again. "Like I was saying, two women"—Snack holds up two fingers—"Apart from my mother—only Megan… and you. Min, I'm so sorry if I ever made you feel not good enough. I don't care about Henry. I know you'd never hurt anyone on purpose, and I don't even really consider what we did cheating now that you've told me the truth."

"But I lied. A lie of omission."

"I've been lying to myself for years. It's easy to do. Min, I've traveled many steps and too many years to get back to the door of your heart. I'm so tired. I was wondering—if I tried knocking, would you let me in? And if you did, could I never leave? I want to be with you. I thought about you even when I was with Me—" Snack's voice catches on his wife's name.

"You can say her name, Snack. Megan. Snack, you just lost your wife. I just... I don't know? Broke up with my... I don't know what Henry was. Wook almost died, we've only gone on one real date, and I haven't talked to you in over a week." Now, I'm just babbling.

Snack paces in front of me, running his fingers through his hair. "I don't fucking care about any of that!"

Oh my God! He's really worked up. He just said fuck again. Snack didn't even stumble on the profanity; he just keeps going.

Snack admonishes himself. "I'm so hard headed! I've been crazy about you since the second I met you. I don't know a time when I didn't love you. Even when I hated you and you hated me, I loved you."

"What about Megan?"

"Minnie, I loved her very much. And she was the mother of my children, but she was a poor imitation for you. That sounds horrible. My kids will *never* know that. People, especially ones that don't know us are going to say it's wrong. Us, together. And Megan's parents? They'll shit kittens, but I'm so lonely. I have been for a while. But not lonely for just anyone. Lonely for you. Please give me another chance. You know me, Min. You're my girl. You've never, not been my girl. I love you." Snack looks at me for some sort of response.

It's what I've been waiting to hear since he first kissed me at Baskin-Robbins. I don't even have the desire to say something smartass, just something true. I grab Snack as he paces in front of me and pull him to me. Cupping his cheeks in my palms, I run them down to his bearded jaw and then his shoulders. Snack bends his head down and our foreheads touch. I close my eyes. "I'm not just your girl. I'm your person. And you're mine. And I love you, too. So, so much."

Then I find Snack's lips and kiss him like it's the first time before I allow his tongue to enter my mouth and glide rhythmically with mine. I moan with happiness and desire.

Snack pulls away. "We don't have to do this right now. That's not what this is about."

"No. I want it to be. It should be." I reassure Snack and then find his mouth again.

Now that there are no more secrets or concealed emotions between us, our kisses are more electric, more devastating. They rip right into my heart and send jolts of passion to my core. Wordlessly, Snack and I undress each other. I pull his chunky navy blue shawl collar cardigan from his shoulders and practically cover Wookiee when I toss it onto the chair.

Wookiee looks up, but puts his head right back down. It's like he's content knowing Snack and I are together.

I run my fingers and hands through Snack's beard and then over his chest.

He exhales raggedly at my touch and kisses me from my ear, down my neck, to my shoulder. Each suckle from his lips amps up my need.

I grasp the hem of Snack's white T-shirt, grazing my fingertips across the skin right above his jeans.

Snack groans. "Oh, God, Minnie." He grabs my ass, pulling me up against him. I feel his insistent hardness through his well-worn jeans. "Again, we have a pants issue."

I shoot him my best come-on smile and he takes it for the invitation it is. He unzips my jeans. They, along with my panties are off and chucked across the room in mere moments. I am naked from the waist down, covered only by my oversized cashmere sweater.

"Goddam, that's sexy as fuck!" Snack breathes in my ear as he lifts one of my legs and pulls it up around his waist. He runs his fingertips up and down my leg and I shiver.

"Wow, I have never heard you use the fuck word like this." I tease him.

"Someone once told me it was very effective. I have come to believe that in the past few minutes."

When I throw my head back in genuine laughter, Snack kisses my neck. One of his hands skates up my side under my sweater. He nimbly removes my bra and cups my breast. I grind my pelvis into his. Snack grabs my other leg and pulls it up around his hip so he's carrying my full weight. He walks toward the bed still kissing me the entire time.

I reach down and grab his T-shirt again. This time successfully pulling it up and over his head, only breaking the deliciousness of his mouth on mine for a nanosecond.

Snack smiles into our kiss. My sweater is removed in the same manner, right before Snack drops me on my back onto the bed.

I lay there, perfectly happy, in nothing but a smile gazing up at the most beautiful man in the world. The only man I've ever loved. Or ever will. And I'm disappointed because he has on far too many clothes.

"Snack," I command, "pants. Make them go away." I point at his crotch.

Snack wastes not a tick. His jeans are off and have joined mine somewhere in the loft. There he is, all of him. I push myself up on my elbows for a better view. My eyes can't stop surveying his body. They move from one gorgeous element of him to the next, taking in the totality of his completely toned, powerful self. I can even get a good look at his tight, muscular ass in the mirror behind him.

Snack must having been doing the same thing because when he finally touches me, our eyes snap to each other. Snack runs his hand from my outer knee up to my inner thigh, dragging his thumbnail along its path. My skin pebbles and all the hairs stand up all over my body. When he reaches the apex of my thighs, he drags his fingers from one hipbone to the next and then back and then finally slips his thumb down, unhooding my clit. From there he circles and circles and I can no longer hold myself up on my elbows.

I fall back and pull in the pleasure. It's so overwhelming I have to close my eyes.

Snack lifts one of my legs to his shoulder and he drops to his knees. He replaces the circular motion of his thumb with his tongue. Round and round, unrelenting. Pausing every few rotations to suck deeply at my clit. I claw at his hair and back when my release overtakes me, and I curl up toward him involuntarily, every muscle in my core clenching.

"Oh my God, oh my God, oh my God!" I chant like a prayer, but Snack doesn't stop. He makes sure I roll through the feeling a few more times before emerging from below. And I didn't have to think about Darth Vader even once! It was all Snack!

Snack crawls up my body with a huge smile across his lips. I reach down and take his cock in one hand and his balls in the other, appreciating the hardness and weighing the heaviness. He groans as I run my thumb cross the plush fullness of the head of his cock. I want to do for him what he just did for me and I make a move to sit up. I can't wait to have him in my mouth, but Snack simply bends down and places his forearms next to my head.

He bites his lip. "No, no time for that, Minnie. If you even breathe on my dick I'll lose it. I need to be in you, like yesterday."

I give no argument and only guide him into me. I'm so wet and ready he slides in easily in two thrusts. Then he stills and I can feel his girth expand even as he's in me. Snack closes his eyes, cocks his head, and sucks his lips together.

"Mmm," he moans. It's like he just tasted something delicious. He looks so happy.

I thrust against Snack and he meets me. We slowly rock into each other until the languid pace is not enough. I grab at his ass and the rhythm becomes pounding, punishing, perfect! I become dizzy as we both orgasm, screaming each other's names, arms grasping for each other.

God, I'm so glad my brothers made me take a shower

and get my shit together!

I'm embarrassed to say I think I may have had that last pair of underwear on for three days. I chuckle to myself.

Snack tried to catch his breath. "What are you laughing about?"

I can't tell him about the dirty panty thing. "Just something Clip said."

Snack smirks. "I don't want to hear it. You said never to listen to him again."

I rest my head on Snack's chest and smile. "He said we were two of the stupidest smart people he ever met."

Snack laughs aloud. It resonates in my ear. "I hate to say it, but in this case, I think Clip is right."

Chapter 24
2014 – The Last Sleepover

Coming downstairs in the morning after our night of confessions and declarations and much more lovemaking wasn't awkward at all. It was perfect.

We slept in so SNACKS is in full swing when we join the café. Snack carries Wookiee, who with the exception of whimpering a bit and needing a pain pill in the middle of the night, was doing fine with the trip to Downers Grove.

Aiden and Fifi come running the minute they see us.

Fifi stops in her tracks at the sight of Wookiee, bandaged and broken, "Oh no, Wookiee. Gil told us he got hurt. Poor baby!"

Wookiee wags his stubby tail and I swear his eyes brightened.

"Can I hold him?"

Snack looks to me and I nod. "Maybe sit down and we'll put him in your lap. We don't want him to fall."

"Good idea." Fifi clambers into one of the café chairs.

Snack places Wookiee on her lap. Fifi kisses him over and over and tells him what a brave boy he is and how much she loves him. Aiden comes over and gives Wookiee the sweetest little boy kiss on the head. They really love my fur boy.

I sit next to Fifi and Wookiee in case he wiggles too much and she needs help.

Snack gets coffee and scones from Colette and comes back to the table. He sits next to Aiden who promptly asks, "Did you have a sleepover?"

Snack smiles and bends down to kiss his son's forehead. "Yes we did, Aiden."

"I'm glad. Sleepovers make you happy. Are you going to stop being sad now?

Nodding while looking at me, Snack tells him, "Minnie makes me happy. And yes, I'm definitely going to stop being sad now."

The door opens and my dad, Sid, Clip, and Jennifer Jacksy enter SNACKS. Dad stops to take Colette's hand and they move over to the table.

Fifi's head has been moving back and forth, carefully monitoring all the elements of the conversation, verbal and non-verbal, when she suddenly chirps, "Are you gonna be my new mom, Minnie?"

The others arrive at the table just as Fifi asks her question. They, each and every one, laugh without reserve.

My jaw drops in disbelief

Snack lets out a huge guffaw. "I can't believe my seven-year-old just proposed to you." But after a beat he adds, "But what do you think?"

Wookiee loudly barks his approval. The first full bark out of him since the accident.

Raising an eyebrow and looking around at all the people I care for most in this world, I say, "I think you have at least one of us sold."

THE END??? (Because is it ever REALLY The End?)

Epilogue
Ten minutes later-Snack

I know just the words I want to say.

"Minnie, you are my best friend. I've loved you since the day we met. I fell in love with you every day since. When we went to college and met other people—I still loved you even though you had made the jump across the hyperspace of time. See what I did there?" Wink.

"But in my heart we were NBU. I love you now in the most impossibly desperate way. Never leave me. I think you and me and Wookiee and Fifi and Aiden make a great team. And I miss having a team. I want a bigger team of little Snacks. Please make me the happiest I could ever be and marry me."

Then I'm gonna kneel down and give her a little chunk of sparkliness in a teal blue box.

Yeah, and I'm probably gonna fucking cry.

What do you think? You think she'll say yes after twenty-six years, three weeks, and eleven hours?

Acknowledgements

Thank you:

Lauren Schmelz and Janine Weathers from the Write Divas. Thank you is not enough. You're tough and thorough and make me work harder and therefore, better.

Oh, and Mr. Lauren – Thanks for the HVAC tip.

Sarah Hansen from Okay Creations. Thank you for my beautiful cover. I don't know how you do it, but you do it right.

Jason and Marina at Polgarus Studios.

My Beta readers: Isabelle, Karrie, Brian, and Theresa .

Anne Wathen, my legal consultant. Thanks for keeping me organized and legal.

My fellow authors/friends and book bloggers, some I've never met in person, but who have inspired and helped me even if they didn't know it:

Isabelle Peterson

Liv Morris

Rachel Robinson

Theresa Troutman

Z.B. Heller

And Jamie McGuire-for your FAQs for Writers page on your website.

The talented authors of BFFS and 101.

And last-the loves of my life, BC, The Connor Boys, and Jasper. You give me the best ideas and lines.

About the Author

Emme Burton is the author of the Better Than Series: Better Than Me, Fix It For Us, and Still Into You. She lives in St. Louis, Missouri with her amazing husband and sons, and her "fur boy." Emme has never, ever been lost in a mall either as a child  or an adult. Her mother, and now her family, have always known where to find her. At the bookstore.

Like Emme's Facebook Page: Author Emme Burton
Follow her on Twitter: @EmmeBurton
Add her books to your TBR on GoodReads.